INTO THE BLOOD

BROKEN OUTLAW SERIES, BOOK TWO

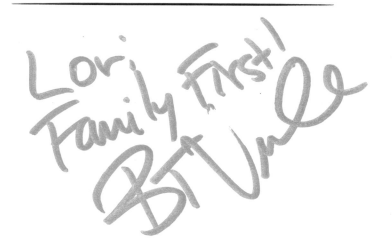

Lori
Family First!
BT Urruela

BT URRUELA

Photographer: Furious Fotog & CJC Photography
Front Cover Model: Tessi Leanne
Back Cover Models: Gideon Connelly, Sam Ashley, Rob Somers & Golden Czermak
Cover Designer: Cover Me Darling
Editor: Proof Before You Publish
Interior Design and Formatting: Champagne Formats

DEDICATION

This book is dedicated to the victims of abuse. Don't ever be ashamed of who you are and don't ever feel ashamed for telling your story. We are victims, yes, but we are also survivors. Share what you've been through, own your strength, and help those still going through it. You can change a life through your honesty.

Warning
This book may contain potential triggers for people who have suffered traumatic experiences. Reader discretion is advised.

PROLOGUE

Xander

Present

"We Fall Apart"—We As Human

"Baby?" I ask, sitting up in bed with the phone to my ear, and reaching over with my other hand to switch the light on.

I can hear her, but nothing she's saying makes sense… just gut-wrenching sobs. She gasps for air between her cries, trying to speak, but nothing comes out.

"Baby, what's wrong? Talk to me, please!" I plead, dropping my head in my hand.

She tries, but she can't. It sounds as if she's choking.

"Paige, baby, please!"

"My dad…" she finally forces out between wretched cries. She doesn't have to say anything else, I already know, and my heart breaks for her. I don't let her finish. She doesn't have to.

"Oh, my god, Paige, I'm so, so sorry." Her crying is

uncontrollable now. It rips my heart right out of my chest. To think I am here, trying to salvage a relationship with my sister when Paige has lost everyone she's ever loved. The guilt is crippling, constricting my chest and making it hard to breathe through the tightness in my throat.

"He...he hung himself. He left a note on the door. I didn't listen...I should've listened," she says, her voice trembling.

She bawls again, mumbling incoherent words. I can hear Irish and Brandi in the background consoling her.

"Baby, don't say another word. I'm coming. I'll hit the road tonight and be there in the morning."

"Xander, honey, you can't," she says, her voice shaking. "Your sister."

"You don't need to worry about that. Baby... I don't even know what to say. I'm so fucking sorry. I'm coming to you. I can't let you do this alone. Not anymore."

She stifles her cries and clears her throat. Speaking with authority this time, she says, "Xander... I love you so much. There's nothing I want more than to be in your arms and to forget any of this ever happened, but it just can't be. First off, Brandi and Chase are here. They've got me. Second, your sister is in trouble. You need to be there for her."

"I need to be there for *you*, Paige!"

"Well... she needs you too. This... this was a long time coming. I fought so hard to break him of his misery. So hard. I guess just not hard enough."

"Paige." I pause, needing so badly to see her beautiful eyes staring back at me. To touch her, hold her and to never let her go again. "I need you," I continue. "I need to see you. I need to know you'll be okay." The realization that Jack is gone sweeps over me, a complete sadness which makes me hurt that much harder for Paige. Though I knew him for only a short time, he had an incredible impact on me. Teresa and Jack showed we what it meant to belong to a real family. And through them, I met Paige, which is something I will forever be grateful for.

"I will be, Xander. Somehow..." I can hear the tears beginning again, but she breathes in deep, fighting them off. "I'm going to bury my father, remove myself from this horrible *fucking* town, and I'll meet you up there." She pauses, taking another long, deep breath. "Baby, I could never give up on us," she says, bringing tears to my eyes. How I wish I could be there with her. "As much as I want to quit right now, as much as that seems like the best way to ease this pain, I know I was put on this earth for you, and you were put on this earth for me. I'll never give up on you because I know you'd never give up on me. We're forever."

"God, Paige," I say, a lump wedging its way into my throat. "I love you so fucking much. You know that?" I ask, wishing there was more I could say. Something stronger. Something that could take it all away, but there's nothing. She is broken, and only time can fix that. Time, and all the fucking love I can give her.

"Of course I know. I love you too, baby. Always and forever," she whispers.

"Always and forever." I pause, my eyes closed and the tears steady now. I breathe through the pain in my chest, knowing immediately what I must do. And knowing without a doubt in this fucking world. "I'll see you soon, baby," I reply, as the line clicks off.

Immediately, I pack my backpack, slip out of the motel

room, and hop on my Harley. With a rumble of the engine and slow roll onto the road, I start the seventeen-hour journey back to Paige, back to the woman I love... to mend her broken heart just as she once mended mine.

CHAPTER ONE

Xander

Two weeks earlier

"Good Man"—Devour the Day

I MISS PAIGE. I'VE MISSED HER DESPERATELY SINCE I TOOK off on the back of this hog a couple of days ago. After being a prisoner for so long, without choices or say, it feels damn good to be on the open road, seeing parts of the country I've never seen before. The endless rows of corn in Kansas; the wide-open nothingness of South Dakota; the rising rocks of western Wyoming gutting the horizon. They're breathtaking, every last one of them. I look upon the God-created beauty and take it all in with a quiet, thankful reserve.

There's not much in the way of life out here as I push my way into northwest Wyoming, on my way to Gabriela's adopted hometown—Trinity. I don't know anything about the town, other than what I could find online, but the consensus is Trinity was a big player in the old days of western expansion... the gold rush days. Back when Native Americans were being bottle-necked onto desperate and dreary reservations and gold was being carelessly pillaged from the virgin land. The area was flooded with the vagrant and vile, the outcasts of society.

Crossing under the large, wrought iron sign welcoming me into Trinity, I can't help but chuckle at the thought of things not being much different than they had been back then. The antique sign gives way to a four-block main street that's stood the test of time well. No building is over two stories high and most look like they weren't built this century. Instead of your typical Starbucks, McDonald's, and Dave & Buster's, none of which can be found a hundred-plus miles in either direction, there's the Creekside Café and Bakery, Wagon Wheel Bar and Grill, and the Six Shooter Saloon—the spot where Irish's friend, Rock, told him Gabriela spends a lot of her time these days.

I pull into the less-than-remarkable Hollywood Starlight Hotel and Casino and hop off my bike, carrying the only thing I bothered to bring with me—my backpack. After getting checked in and dropping off my shit, I head down to the bar for a beer. I've managed to keep my drinking to a minimum since being out, but after half a day on these isolated Wyoming roads, I'm in need of a buzz and some conversation.

I down two beers in quick succession while making my daily call to Paige. She doesn't sound so well, and I know her father is suffering. The whole situation makes it that much harder to be away from her. She swears she's getting by okay, and that Irish and Brandi have been there with her every step of the way, but it doesn't make me feel any less guilty for being away from her. I just need to make my connection with Gabriela, do my best to make things right with her, to keep her out of trouble, and then I'm on my way back home, back to my girl, back where I belong.

After one last beer at the hotel bar, I head over to the Six Shooter Saloon, which feels a lot like stepping back in time. There are the classic wooden swinging doors that give way to three aged poker tables on my left as I walk into the saloon. A handful of weathered bearded gentlemen sit around the tables and look up from their cards with inquisitive, judging glances. They eventually tire of me, and return to their game, as I grab a stool at the bar. The bartender, with filthy overalls, a cutoff tee, and a warm smile, motions to me.

"What'll it be, partner?" He flips a dirty rag over his shoulder and leans an elbow against the bar.

"That Devil's Hatchet pale ale any good?"

He chuckles and shakes his head. "You're askin' the wrong guy. I don't drink that shit. People seem to like it though. It's local. I think all that shit tastes like fuckin' urine."

"You know what urine tastes like?" I laugh, and he just shrugs.

"I've had it a time or two. It's sterile, ya know?" He sports a crooked smile, pulling at a spotty blonde beard not to be proud of, and I can't help but think he may actually be telling me the truth.

"Well shit, give me some of that urine then, please."

He winks and clicks his tongue. "Coming right up, partner."

Turning his back to me, he grabs a pint glass and starts to fill it. I glance around the room, noting a handful of rough-looking men playing pool on the other end of the bar and engaged in loud conversation, two more lonesome souls seated at the bar with me, and the men with dirty glances playing cards at the table. I look back to the bartender as he places the beer before me, foam spilling over the edges of the glass.

"You aren't from here, are you?" I ask, and he grunts.

"Whatcha thin' gives it away?" he asks, thickening his twang.

Through a chuckle, I ask him, "Where's home?"

"Well…" He lifts two palms in the air and looks around. "This *is* home. Been in Trinity the better part of fifteen years. Born and raised 'Bama though. Family's from Winfield."

"Ah, I've never been. I'm a Florida man myself." He rolls his eyes and reaches under the counter, pulling out a Crimson Tide hat and slipping it on. He takes his time positioning it just right with a smirk on his face.

I roll my eyes, brushing him off, and then I lean forward into the bar. "So, if you've been here awhile, do you know if a Gabriela Michaels will be in tonight? Or if this is the right place to find her?" I ask. He raises an eyebrow, a look of doubt passing over him.

"Gabi? Yeah, she's in here damn near every other night. Not sure about tonight though. How do you know her?" His sudden intrigue has me regretting I asked.

"She's an old friend of mine. I heard she moved back here after the Army, so I came to surprise her." I come up with the first thing that touches my brain, and he seems to buy it.

"Shit, I didn't think Gabi had any friends." He laughs.

"Do you know her well?" I ask.

"That, I do. I used to be best friends with her pop before he passed. Good man. Fuckin' awful drunk, but when he was sober, the bastard took real good care of 'em. That is until Dotty went. Did ya know the Michaels's?"

"No, I never got the chance to meet them. Gabriela always spoke very highly of them though," I say, playing along.

"Gabriela, huh? I thought I heard ya wrong the first time. Y'all must be *real* good friends. The last time I called her that, she damn near broke a beer bottle over my head." He laughs and flips two shot glasses over onto the bar. "Shot?"

I hesitate, knowing full well I don't need a shot, but also understanding these kinds of things aren't passed on between men. "Sure, what are you having?"

"Does it matter?" He laughs and pulls a bottle from behind the bar. "Jack Daniels has my 'Bama heart. Hope you're okay with that cause it's what yer gettin." He chuckles as he pours the shots and then stows the bottle.

"I'm a Jameson man myself, but Jack will do just fine." I lift the shot glass. "Cheers." We take the shots and the striking sweetness of the Jack burns all the way down. He lifts the glass toward me, nodding, and then makes his way back down the bar.

As I toss my beer back in hopes of ridding my taste buds of the Jack, I catch Gabriela walk up to the bar in my peripheral. Had I not looked her up beforehand, I would have never known it was her, though the resemblance is striking. Lowering the beer, I notice she scans the area behind her intently as the man with her greets the bartender with a hand shake. The familiarity in her features catches me off guard for a moment, and I stare, the only thing crossing my mind is her as a two year old, crying from the crib... and me unable to help her, no matter how hard I tried.

CHAPTER TWO

Gabriela

"Raise Hell"—Dorothy

"A BOUT DAMN TIME, ASSHOLE." I DAB OUT MY CIGARETTE on the Six Shooter's wooden siding as Shane approaches through dusk's dimming light, ten minutes late, as he so often is. He's wearing his patented smile, equipped with dimples that could make any woman's knees weak. Not mine though. I've known those damn dimples for far too long now. They worked on me long ago, but I can fight them off these days. Besides, I'm not the swooning type. He'd get off on that too much.

He pulls off his fedora and bows with it.

"Hey, have you come to expect anything less from me?" he asks, standing back straight, and returning the hat to his head. He greets me with a hug, wrapping his thick arms around me. He's about the only man I can even stomach touching me anymore and his arms still carry the same electric sense of security they always have. If I cared enough to love someone, I mean to *truly* love someone without reservations... this man would be the one.

"You know, the whole basic training deal is supposed to break you of that habit. How did you manage to miss that?" I ask him as I make my way through the bar doors, Shane close behind.

"If I didn't have a battle buddy in basic as prompt and perky in the morning as you were, I think it would've stuck a little better. So, I blame you," he says with a coy little smile. I scoff, my lip rearing back into the look of judgmental disgust I so often carry. For him, at least, it's just a pretend one. The same can't be said for most everybody else.

We take two seats at the bar and I'm relieved to not see Javi in here playing pool like he usually is, but some of his minions are. *Fuck them.* I should probably be avoiding this place with the predicament I'm in, but that's not my style. I refuse to be afraid, or to show my fear at the very least. It's not in my nature. They're sure to come by eventually, and I'm sure to get an earful. At this point, an earful is the least of my concerns.

"If it weren't for me," I continue, "they would've sent your ass back to Jersey before you even got your uniform. Just thank me, Shane." I glance around the bar behind me as Shane greets Jimmy. Satisfied I won't be getting fucked with just yet, I lean into the bar, nodding at Jimmy who greets us with two Buds in his hands. "And shut the fuck up," I snap at Shane, a pretend scowl taking up my face.

He pulls back, faking a look of shock before tossing his fresh beer back. He plops the bottle down on the bar top and removes his fedora, setting it down next to it.

"You're lucky I like you. I'm not afraid to hit a woman," he jokes.

"Oh, how quickly we forget who beat whose ass in combatives. Don't make me refresh your memory." I think back to that time, nearly five years ago, when we were just two young and dumb privates in basic training learning the Army ropes. I did, in fact, kick his ass in combatives and neither the drill sergeants, nor our fellow recruits, ever let him live it down. It was a whole different world back then. I had so much hope… so much optimism for the future.

Five years and a shortened military career later and here I am with more hate in my heart than I thought I could ever possess, and on the brink of my body being hacked up into a hundred little pieces and thrown into Snake River.

"How many times do I have to remind you?" He looks away, trying his best to fight a smile from taking up his face. "I let you win," he finishes, finally cracking up.

"You have got to be shitting me, Shane. You're still gonna stick to that story, huh? Even though there were plenty of witnesses who can verify you having been annihilated by a woman."

"Yeah, well the only one you still talk to from basic is me, so what do you got now?"

"You're a fucking idiot." I roll my eyes and put two fingers up for Jimmy to come back around.

"What can I get ya, darlin'? Same thing?" Jimmy asks.

"Yeah, and two shots of Cuervo, Jimmy." He looks surprised as he readies the shot glasses.

"Cuervo? I see it's gonna be one of them nights, huh?" He laughs and fills them. He then nods down the bar to an attractive man sitting by himself and cradling a beer. I look to him, observe, and then look back at Jimmy.

"Guy came in here askin' bout ya when he first sat down. Says he's an old friend. Now, I may not know ya as well as I think I do, but since when do ya have old friends. Or friends of any kind for that matter? You're about as friendly as a rattle-snake on spin cycle." He lets out a roar of laughter as only he can. Anyone else makes a noise like that in here and everyone in the damn bar will be staring, but not Jimmy. We've all heard that obnoxious laugh of his more times than can be counted.

"No shit?" I analyze the stranger at the bar again. He looks normal enough. Nothing that would make me think he's with Javi's crew, but he doesn't look like military either.

"Thanks, Jimmy. Appreciate it."

"Need me to get rid of him?" he asks.

"No, no, you're good. I think I remember him," I lie.

CHAPTER THREE

Xander

"Narrow Mouth"—The Early November

I've been trying to work up the courage to talk to her since they sat down, but I can't for the life of me think of something that would sound halfway normal. I've thought about telling her I was in the Army too, but I don't know enough about her military past to pull that one off. I could tell her I was stationed at Fort Lewis with her, but then what if she starts asking questions? I don't know shit about the base. I also wasn't expecting her to be with someone. Hell, I've already waited twenty-some-odd years to talk to her. One night longer or fifty isn't going to make much of a difference.

Finishing up the last of my beer and ready to call it quits for the night, I no longer have a choice. I feel them both approach on my left, and I pretend to not see them standing there. Uncomfortable, I eventually look and see Gabi eyeing me inquisitively. The man she's with stands behind her with his arms crossed and eyes flitting around the room, studying it.

"So, Jimmy here says you were looking for me. Says you know me." She leans in a little, her eyes saying don't-fuck-with-me. "But I don't know who the fuck you are and that's a problem."

I don't say anything for a moment. I wasn't really prepared for this, though I've had weeks to get ready. I want to give her the truth, I really do, but every bit of hesitation in the world has the truth securely buried.

"I was Army. And we have a mutual friend. I mentioned stopping up here to him and he suggested linking up with you. Said you might have the good stuff," I rattle off, barely registering what's coming out.

"No, I used to have the good stuff." She turns back to the guy with her and chuckles, but it seems caused more by nerves than anything else. "But not anymore. Army, huh?" Her eyes trail down my body, sizing me up. "You don't look like a military guy."

"I've been out for a while. If I don't look like former military that means I'm doing something right. I'm trying to forget that life," I say with a laugh. She scoffs and shakes her head.

"Tell me about it. And we know some of the same people?" she asks.

"Yeah…well, one person at least. Rock Callahan. We went to basic together. My name's Chase. Chase McGregor." The lie comes off my tongue as fluid as if it were the truth, and I'm silently impressed with myself. Her mouth forms a wide O. She looks back at the guy with her and then to me again. He now has the same look on his face. He takes a step forward, nudging Gabi to the side.

"Wait a second. Irish? You're Irish *fucking* McGregor?"

Fuck me. "That's me. I guess my reputation precedes me?"

"Shit, I guess so. Rock and I are boys. I did two tours with that motherfucker." He points to Gabi and then back at himself. "We both did. She did another one with him after that." He's got a shit-eating grin on his face now, which is vastly different than the smoldering glare he came at me with before. "Rock used to always talk about this guy Irish from basic training who used to own that shit. Said the guy was a fucking wrecking ball. I always thought you'd be bigger." He laughs and I do the same, trying whatever I can to keep up with the ruse.

"I'm Shane, by the way." He puts out his hand, and I shake it. His shake is firm, almost to the point of pain. It's one of those tough guy handshakes. I don't mind though. For all I know he's with Gabi and thinks I might be trying to encroach. The disgusting irony behind that thought is jarring.

"And I'm Gabi, though I take it you already knew that. Fuck Rock for putting my name out there like that. Fucking asshole. He wants to bitch at me about selling H and then sends me business?" She laughs, shaking her head from side to side. "Fucking redneck Asians. They can't be trusted."

"Oh shit, I wasn't looking for heroin," I say. "Just some greenery to get me by while I'm up here for work."

"Greenery? You mean smoke? You said the good stuff, I was thinking you meant the harder shit," she says, pulling back a stool and taking a seat. Shane stands just behind her with his hands on her shoulders.

"I got a whole bunch back at Gabi's place. I can probably hook you up," Shane says and Gabi shoots a glare back at him.

"Inviting strangers over to *my* place, dickhead?"

"He went to basic with Rock! *Our* Rock," Shane argues.

"Hey, it's all good. I can look elsewhere. Just thought I'd ask," I say, motioning the bartender to bring my tab. I set two twenties on the bar for him.

"No, it's all good. Just giving you shit. Rock is a good friend of ours," she says and turns back to Shane again. "We should probably get out of here before Javi and the rest of his crew get here anyway. I've had enough to drink." She throws some cash on the bar too as the barkeep collects mine and she lifts herself from the stool.

"Jimmy, settle me out," she says.

"You got it, darlin'," he responds before his eyes dart to the opening bar doors, concern growing on his face. My focus shifts right along with his. "*Fuck me*," he mumbles.

She looks over as a group of guys who look like nothing but trouble come walking in. Shane turns, keeping Gabi behind him as the new arrivals beeline toward us.

"Are you really that fucking stupid, Gabi? I mean, really?" the obvious leader of the group asks, his guys behind him looking like they're ready to fuck some shit up. The handful of guys who were playing pool before now make their way over.

"I was just grabbing a drink, Javi. We're leaving now." She collects up her change and leaves a five on the bar.

"Hmmmm." He puts his hand to the dark scruff taking up his chin, scratches, and studies Gabi. "Funny that you're in *my* fucking bar, spending *my* fucking money. Does that make sense to you?"

Jimmy clears his throat, leaning over the bar a bit. "It's actually my bar, Javi." He flashes a slanted smile and Javi shoots him a death stare without a word. Jimmy puts both hands up and backs away slowly. "But hey, man, mi casa, su casa. Ya know what I mean?"

Javi looks back to Gabi and smirks. "So?"

"Javi, this is the only decent place in town. You know that. And I only had a few." She stands her ground, but there's new nervousness taking up her voice. Javi takes two steps forward, face to face with Gabi, and nudging Shane out of the way in the process.

"Do you think I'm *fucking* joking here? You think this is a *fucking* game? You've got three more weeks. Three fucking weeks to get me my money." He jabs a finger in her face. "You better save every fucking dime you got." Shane's face contorts in noticeable anger, the veins in his neck throbbing.

"Hey, we're fucking leaving, man. Just get the fuck out of our way," Shane says, putting Gabi behind him again. He takes a step forward, but Javi doesn't move.

"And who the fuck are you, cowboy? Here to save the day?" Javi looks back at his guys and then again to Shane with a wide smile on his face. "I'll tell you what, hero. If I don't see my money, I'll skin you alive too. Sound good?" he asks as one of his men pulls out a bowie knife and traces its sharp blade with his thumb.

Shane looks like he's about to explode, but Gabi grabs his arm and pulls.

"Shane, please, let's just go," she pleads, tugging a few more times for good measure. He reluctantly follows, while Javi and his men remain as still as they've been the entire time.

"Yeah, little Shane, listen to your whore," Javi calls out from the side of his mouth. "Go home. Don't go getting yourself into trouble. She's in enough of it for the both of you." He flashes a wicked smile, exposing a flashy yellow gold grill. Shane looks back once more before letting Gabi guide him out the door. I follow suit, looking Javi dead in the eyes as I pass and he sneers at me, an evil in his eyes I haven't seen since prison. It seems she's in more trouble than Irish let on... or maybe more than he even knew.

CHAPTER FOUR

Gabriela

"Stranger in a Room"—Sara Hartman

THERE'S SOMETHING ODDLY FAMILIAR ABOUT THIS CHASE guy. Something settling. As he leans back into the couch handling a beer, I lick the end of a joint and roll it together. Shane has a beer in his hand as well and his other hand on my leg as it so often goes when he's had a few too many. The poor man. He loves me. He loves every bit of me, flaws and all. And if my bleeding heart could feel a thing, I'd love him right back. I want to. I just can't. I haven't been with a man in three years… and the last time wasn't by choice. I just can't even think about it.

But in a perfect world, he is my perfect counterpart.

"So, what's up with that guy? If you don't mind me asking," Chase asks, his eyes glued on the joint like a hungry dog as I light it. I look over, my eyes meeting Shane's, and I shake my head.

"Ah, he's just a fucking cockroach," I mutter, smoke passing between my lips. I hand Shane the joint and focus my attention back onto our visitor. "So, you see much of Rock these days? What's he been up to?"

"A little bit here and there…" His voice trails as he takes the joint from Shane and hits it. "It's been awhile though."

"He's down there in Vegas still, isn't he?" I ask.

"I'm not too sure, actually. I only spoke with him briefly the other day. We didn't really have a lot of time to catch up," our guest says, holding on to the J entirely too long.

"Hey, stop Bogarting. Puff, puff, pass." I stand, retrieving the joint from Chase's hand and flashing him a smile before plopping back down on the couch.

"Yeah, babe, Rock's still in Vegas busting kneecaps and working the young boys down at The Male Box," Shane says as I straddle my legs over his, lying back into the pillows. He takes off my shoes and rubs his hands firmly against my feet.

"Shit, I haven't seen him in a minute," Shane continues, grabbing a bottle of lotion from the coffee table. "He's a damn good dude."

"You said he served with you guys?" he asks.

"Yeah, with Gabriela in Afghanistan twice," Shane answers for me as I'm currently being put to fucking sleep. God, his hands are gifts from God. And the boy sure knows how to use them. "I was with them on the first one to Afghanistan, and a short stint to Iraq before that," he continues.

"You still in?" Chase asks.

"Nah, I got out after Afghanistan," Shane says, my eyes opening again and following the changes in his facial expressions. I know where his mind is going. That was a tough tour for all of us, we lost a whole lot of guys in the Korengal Valley, but for Shane, it was something else, something else entirely. His best friend Lucas stepped on a landmine right in front of him. Not ten feet away. I was lucky enough to have stayed back on base that mission, but I heard the horror story from our squad afterward.

They said he was picking pieces of Lucas off his uniform for thirty minutes after it happened, just dazed and staring off into the nothing.

He hasn't been the same since.

"I just had enough," Shane continues, interrupting my straying thoughts. "Ended up in Seattle working the fishing docks. It's incredible, let me tell ya," Shane jokes. "What about you? When did you get out?"

"I transitioned about a year and a half ago. Started my own carpentry business. I race a little bit here and there too," Chase says, dabbing the roach out in the ashtray on the coffee table and then melting back into the loveseat.

"Ever deploy?" Shane asks, his hands now working their way up my calves. I close my eyes again and it's a good thing, because they're currently rolling in the back of my head.

"Yeah, once to Iraq. Twice to Afghanistan. Got shot in the ass on my last deployment and separated soon after. Same as you, I just got sick of the grind. When did you get out, Gabi? Or is it Gabriela? I've heard both now," Chase asks and my head jerks up, my gaze narrowing on him.

"*Gabi*," I say sternly, and then grin, lying back into the pillow.

"Yeah, I'm the only one that gets to call her Gabriela. And it took me years to get that privilege," Shane says, tickling my side. I scrunch in, my abs constricting, and an onslaught of giggle fits push their way out.

"Stop it!" I laugh, swatting at his hand. "I never gave you permission, cum stain."

"Cum stain? My filthy mouthed little infantrywoman busting out the cum stain. I haven't heard that one from you in a while, my dear," Shane says, a broad smile on his face. "And you didn't need to give me permission. You'll always be my little Gabriela," Shane continues, blocking his nuts from the fist he knows is sure to come. Lucky for him my entire body is in an all-out buzz, and moving right now seems highly unlikely.

Shane looks at Chase, who is sprawled out on the loveseat himself, and says, "So I started calling her Gabriela because it bothered her so much and, well, it never quite stopped bothering her... so I never quite stopped using it." He chuckles. "Now, it's just weird to even hear someone call her Gabi, let alone say it."

"So, what are you doing down here?" Chase asks and instantly Shane looks down at me.

"I'm just visiting Gabi and I do some work up in Cody here and there. Just got back in town from a job tonight actually," he says before nodding to me. "I think she missed me."

"Fat chance," I say, though I certainly did. I always do when he's gone.

Shane looks back to Chase, whose eyes have taken on a comical shade of red. "I try and visit her every chance I get."

Liar.

It was six months since I saw him last before I rang him a couple weeks ago, begging him for help. He was straddling his Harley and on the road in the time it took me to hang up. He's always been like that with me and it's something I'll always appreciate about him. He is the kindest man I've ever met... and he's all I have.

"Anyway, man," Shane says, removing my legs from his and standing. I pout in protest. "I'm tired as shit, and Gabriela here is looking like she's straight outta Chinatown." He turns to Chase and points. "You don't look so good yourself."

"Feel free to sleep on the couch if you want. Or don't. Up to you," I say, standing as well and feeling Shane's hands meet my waist.

"That would be really great. I'm tired as fuck. I appreciate it," Chase says, as I retrieve a pillow and blanket from a hall closet and toss them on the couch.

"Brunch tomorrow?" I suggest, more statement than question, and without waiting for a response I flip the light switch and follow Shane down the hall. I hear a mumbled response, but can't make it out. At this point, I'm too damn tired to care. I need to feel the warmth of this man's arms. I need to feel safe, or as safe as I'm able to feel, as I fight to get to sleep.

Shane and I had an interesting dynamic, even as far back as basic. I was one of two females in the entire damn thing. I aspired to be the first ever to go Special Forces, which was a recipe for making enemies. And I made a lot of them. Everyone did their best to knock me off course, everyone except Shane. They did everything in their power to ensure I wouldn't make the cut, but not him. He stood by me the whole way, talked me down from the ledge when I needed it, and backed me up when the snide remarks and name calling turned to full on hazing. I proved them all wrong though, and I worked my ass off to do it, but I don't know if I could've done it without Shane.

He was my battle buddy, and more than that, he was my

cheerleader. Always fighting for me. Always lifting me up when I wanted to quit. What started as a great friendship eventually led to something more... feelings for him that swept in out of nowhere and completely overwhelmed me. In the height of our time spent in combat during our deployment to Iraq, we found ourselves yearning for more. Sometimes it was physical, but most of the time, he would just sneak into my bunk and cuddle with me on my cot until I drifted to sleep, and then he'd sneak back out before anyone could spot us. We found comfort in each other during a time when death was always looming, and in that, he did what many before him could not do.

He tore down my walls.

Oftentimes when I'm cradled in his arms like this, with his rough thumb trailing my body from thigh to neck and back, I'm brought back to those desperate days in the desert when his touch was the only thing that helped me to forget.

CHAPTER FIVE

Xander

"Wish You Were Here"—Lower Than Atlantis

"WAIT..." PAIGE GIGGLES, AN EARLY MORNING RASP IN her voice that makes my fucking dick buzz. "Why did you tell her you were Chase, baby?" I shake my head, looking out on the street from the front porch.

"Babe, how the fuck do you go up to someone like 'hey, long lost brother here. How ya been, sis?'...I panicked. The bartender mentioned I was asking about her and I was pretty much shit out of luck after that."

"Oh, Xander." She giggles again and it makes me ache to be there with her, waking up in bed with my Baileys and coffee, holding her until morning turns to midday. It would be just what I need right now. "I miss you so much," she says as if she were reading my thoughts.

"God, I miss you too. Has it really only been four days? It's felt like forever."

"You have no idea..." Her voice trails and she sighs loudly

into the phone. "So what's she like?" she asks.

"She's really cool, actually. A total badass. Foul mouthed like Brandi." I laugh and she does too, and it's almost as if we are actually together. I close my eyes to hold on to that feeling as long as I can.

"A guy from her unit, an old friend I guess, is here with her. Good dude. Quiet. He's definitely got an I've-killed-people-for-a-living look." She laughs loudly into the phone as I hear her rustling under her covers. "I think we ran into the trouble Chase was talking about last night too."

"Really?" she asks.

"Yeah, some hard-looking dudes. Pretty much clones of what I saw in prison. I'm going to try and get as much on the situation as I can while the whole impersonation thing lasts." My thoughts trail to Chase and how he may feel about what I'm doing. I'm quite certain he wouldn't be happy about it. "Hey, babe," I say. "Would you mind keeping this quiet with Brandi and Irish for now? I want to tell him myself."

"Yeah, of course, love. I won't say anything."

"Hey, you know I don't want to ask, but I feel like I have to. I just worry, baby," I say, quietly, noticing movement inside through the large front window.

"Dad's okay," she says, obviously knowing full well where I was going with it. "We're just taking it one day at a time." Her voice is low, apprehensive.

"Well, you know I'm here for you if you need it," I say, waving to Gabi as she walks by the window. "Baby, they're up and moving now. I think we're going to go out to breakfast in a bit. I'll give you a call here a little later though, okay?"

"Okay, babe. Sounds perfect."

I pause, swallowing stiffly as the weight of what she's going through hits me. "If you need anything, baby… anything at all. You call me and I'm there in a heartbeat."

"I know, Xander," she says, sweetly. "I'm okay. I promise. I love you so, so much."

"I love you too, Paige. I'll talk to you soon." I press end on the iPhone, holding it in my hands for a moment and just closing my eyes, painfully wishing I could be in two places at once.

The opening of the front door pulls my attention and I see Gabi lean out, decked out in last night's band tee with her mess of blonde hair held up by a hair tie on the top of her head.

"Hey, killer, you ready for some fucking bloodys? I'm dying here." She laughs, pretending to choke herself out.

"Yeah, let's do it. I'm starving."

"You never said last night, how long do you plan on staying in the area?" Gabi asks, chasing a forkful of eggs with a long drink of her Bloody Mary. My mind runs through the scenario, but I honestly hadn't even thought about how long I'd stay here. As long as it took to make sure she was okay. So, who the fuck knows how long that'll be.

"I'll be up here a month or so." My mind formulates the lies, on the spot and quickly, as it so often does. "I make this trip once a year. My Wyoming stuff sells the best, so I end up grabbing a lot of shit from up here and shipping it back down."

"Carpentry you said, right? What, like cabinets and shit?" Shane asks, handling a mug of coffee.

"Not really cabinets. More craft type shit. Wine stoppers,

book holders, pens, cutting boards… pretty much anything like that you can think of. Pays well and I love the work." I can almost feel Irish speaking through me.

"Well…" Gabi looks at Shane, pinching his arm and leaning into him. "Shane and I were talking last night, and if you're going to be here that long, there's no reason you should have to pay for a hotel room. Once Shane here…" she nudges him with her elbow, "…clears the band shit out of the way in the guest room, you can just crash on the futon in there."

"Wait, are you sure? I don't want to impose," I say, genuinely shocked.

"Yeah, I wouldn't offer if I didn't mean it." She winks. "Honestly, Rock is a real good friend of ours. He's like family. So a friend of his is a friend of ours. And according to Shane, he's talked quite a lot about you."

"A whole lot," Shane adds with a laugh, raising his cup of coffee in a half cheers.

"Well, that's definitely appreciated. It does get crazy expensive," I say, gathering my change and sliding the server's book to the edge of the table, still trying to believe my own damn luck.

As the world crumbles around me for everyone I love, somehow the luck falls on me, and I couldn't feel worse about it.

"Wait… when the fuck did you get the check?" Gabi asks, looking from the server's book, to the incoming waitress and then back to me.

"I'm sneaky as fuck." I laugh, wiping my mouth with a napkin and tossing it to the table.

"Well… thanks," Gabi says, Shane nodding in agreement.

"No problem at all. So… tell me more about this band shit," I say and Shane's eyes light up.

"You play?" Shane asks.

"Yeah, guitar. And I sing a little bit. You?"

Gabi rolls her eyes and chuckles. "Here we go."

"I play a little guitar and drums, but bass is my shit. I've been playing since I was a kid. I've got all three in the room though." His eyes drift to Gabi and he smiles. The way they look at each other is something else. It takes my mind to Truman Valley, and to the love that is waiting for me there.

"Which Gabriela just fucking loves," Shane says, nudging two knuckles into her side and garnering a squeal. She rears a knee up and then stomps down on his foot. He leans back in obvious pain, biting his lip to keep from making a sound.

"Fuck, woman. That shit hurt," he says through an exhale, attempting to reach down and massage the pain out of his foot. Gabi turns to me with a mischievous smile.

"Yeah, instruments, cords, picks, songbooks… fucking everywhere," she says, with a quick eye roll. "He's been storing his shit at my house for a year now. It's been delightful. 'Just a month' he says. 'I swear I'm moving to Wyoming' he says." Gabi shoots Shane a playful smirk and then huffs dramatically.

Shane shakes off the pain and passes her an exaggerated look of detest. "I'm gonna get you. You know that, right?"

"Uh huh," Gabi responds.

"As long as you know that," Shane says before turning his attention to me. "Anyway, we should definitely jam sometime. Gabriela's neighbors fucking *love* it," Shane jokes, sliding out of the booth before Gabi can get another good stomp in. He puts his hat on and waits with a smile, his arms crossed and a safe distance away, as Gabi and I slide out after him.

"Yeah, it's a fucking dream to deal with them the next day.

Let me fucking tell you." She laughs, swinging a fist down just to the point of hitting Shane in the nuts before stopping. He jerks, flailing his arms in defense as she gingerly walks to the door, a maniacal little giggle trailing behind her.

CHAPTER SIX

Gabriela

"Shame"—Ciaran Lavery

COUNTING SHEEP. IT'S WHAT I DO MOST NIGHTS OUT HERE IN *the desert. After two previous deployments, each one more unbearable than the last, sleep has become a hot commodity. One I don't run into very often. We got in from mission not two hours ago, so the events of the day still play fresh in my head. Tomorrow, it's back to work. Tonight, it consumes me.*

A child, barely four, is caught in the line of fire, his innocent eyes look at me, confused. His mother screams for him to come back, selflessly running after him into the carnage.

I could do nothing but watch from behind the wall as his head split in two from a stray round. His innocent eyes no more. As his tiny body crumpled to the ground, his mother fell onto him, cradling what was left of his head, sobbing in deep, breathless cries that overpowered even the gunfire. She too caught a round, and then another and another. And then she curled into a ball around him... and they became one.

These are the thoughts that race through my mind as wind whips sand against the thin trailer walls. There's no one here but me. No one here to talk to, because unlike every other Special Forces soldier in my unit, and every other SF unit for that matter, I am a woman. And I never had a fucking clue just what that would entail. As tears run freely down my cheeks onto my pillow-case, I wish for only my mother to talk to, to hold me, to tell me everything is going to be okay. I love my guys, they mean the world to me, but sometimes a girl just needs her mother. Regardless of where I am, I won't ever again see mine, but that doesn't mean I don't remember the rock that she was, or the insight she instilled.

Sometimes at night, when I close my eyes just tight enough, and wish for just long enough, I can almost hear her voice telling me I'll be okay. I can almost feel her tender arms wrapped around me, rocking me to sleep.

And then I open my eyes and reality hits, I am a soldier, fighting for a cause I don't believe in, with brothers I would die for. I'm okay with most of that, but it doesn't mean it doesn't fuck with me.

My random fleeting thoughts are interrupted by a light rap at the door.

"Michaels, we got a mission," a muffled voice says through the door. The voice is familiar, but it's too indistinct to be sure who it belongs to. I climb out of bed and slip my pants on. I creep through the dark trailer to the door, flipping the lights on before opening it. My vision is hazy, but the last thing I make out are masked faces and I hear the whir of a stun gun. And then I'm out.

I wake up several times to the same things—sweat, grunting, laughing, and a familiar smell. Not just familiar. Distinct. It's Old Spice aftershave. It's Captain Anderson's Old Spice aftershave. I can't be sure that it's him because every time my eyes open and I fight through the haze enough to see, I get shocked again. And then the darkness envelops me.

I open them again and it's someone else now—thrusting and moaning and taking. Violating. The pain runs through me like blood through veins. And again, I'm shocked by the stun gun, left to the darkness.

My eyes shoot open, my head pounding, and a persistent ache roots itself in my gut. I lift my head from the sweat-soaked pillow and run an arm across my forehead. My heart pounds like a drum in my chest and for a moment, I must tell myself it's not real; that I'm not back in Afghanistan, that I'm not again losing the last piece of myself left that's good.

I rub a palm into each eye letting out a loud groan. There's only one thing that'll ease the hate and pain I feel after nightmares like that and it's hidden in my nightstand drawer. I open it and dig inside, eventually pulling out a locked cash pouch. Standing from my bed, I slink to the bathroom with it.

Standing hunched over the bathroom sink, I unlock the pouch and pocket the key before pulling out its contents; a little baggy of cocaine and a queen of hearts to cut it with. I dab a mound of coke out onto the counter, and using the card, I cut the clumps up into three fine lines, licking my lips in anticipation. Snagging a dollar from my pocket, I roll it and ready it against my nostril, the right one this time as the left has taken a pounding lately.

Just as I'm about to kill the first line in one fell swoop, the bathroom door comes ripping open. I turn and freeze with the bill to my nose, unable to react as I spot Chase wide-eyed with the door hanging half open.

"What the fuck, Chase?!" I yell, impulsively, a snarl on my face.

"Oh, my God," he gasps. "I'm so fucking sorry. I thought I heard you guys leave. Fuck, I'm sorry," he pleads, yet he still stands there with the damn door open as if I'm *not* about to snort fucking coke off a countertop. I straighten, pocketing the bill, and turning to block the lines with my body as he pulls the door closed.

Retrieving the rolled dollar from my pocket again, I take down each line like a fucking hoover. Once they've disappeared, I lick my finger and collect the remaining powder with it before rubbing it into my gums. As I do, my gaze fixates on my reflection in the mirror, tracing the thin lines of my face, the weary, distant look in my eyes, the weathered bags beneath them. I am who I am. As to who that actually is, I'm not so sure anymore. I shake it off, wiping my nose of any evidence. I exit the bathroom just in time to catch Chase hightailing it toward the front door. As I approach him, he fumbles with his keys.

"If you need to use the bathroom, it's available," I say with a smirk.

"I really am sorry. I had no idea you were still here," he says, his eyes on the floor. "A week here and I'm already fucking shit up."

"Hey, listen, it's all good. Shit happens… but whatever you saw in there…" My voice trails as I wait for him to look up. He does with his hand hanging on the door handle. "Keep it between us. Shane doesn't need to know."

His forehead wrinkles in confusion. "No problem at all. I didn't see shit. But I have to ask, what's the big deal? He doesn't really seem like the judgmental type. I used to dabble in the stuff myself. It's no big thing." He shrugs.

"Let's just say I like the powder a little too much some-times." I laugh, though there's nothing funny about it. It's just not something I want to be discussing with him. And it's definitely not something I want to talk to Shane about. He wouldn't let me live it down until I stopped again. If I even get the chance to stop.

He nods. "Hey, I get it. I've had the same relationship with alcohol," he says, smiling.

Before I can respond, the sound of loud banging against the door rips through the small house. Chase pulls his hand back from the handle, looking at me with a puzzled expression. He may not know the devil that stands on the other side of this door, but I do, and it scares the ever-loving piss out of me. Another round of knocking stirs me into action.

"Do you have a gun?" I whisper and he nods. "Grab it and stow it." He nods again and makes his way into the guest room as the banging continues, and I make out Javi yelling from the other side.

"I know you're in there, bitch. Open the fucking door. It's payday," he says. I can barely make out the words as I grab one of my many guns from a kitchen drawer; a small chrome snub nose I stuff into my bra.

"*Open the fucking door,*" he growls. I have no trouble mak-ing that one out. He bangs the door so hard it seems as if it may bust from the hinges at any moment.

Chase comes out from the guest room, stuffing his own pistol into his waistband. He positions himself in the kitchen, behind the counter, and with a clear view of the front door.

"Gabi, please don't make me wait," I hear Javi say, calmer

this time. "You really don't want to push your luck more than you already have."

I press myself against the door, a shaking hand against the deadbolt as I look nervously toward Chase. He nods his head confidently at me, though his eyes tell a different story. I've been in combat, and that's one thing, but to be out here as a civilian, fighting the same kind of ruthless motherfuckers without a hundred other soldiers watching your back... it's a different story entirely. I can feel my life clock tick-tick-ticking down.

I turn the deadbolt and then the bottom lock and open the door, slowly. Reluctantly. Javi stands, bobbing his foot impatiently with the same two hard, ugly-looking motherfuckers he always has with him mean-mugging me from behind him. They're probably six five, maybe six six, but right now they look about eight feet tall. I know anytime I see these guys it may be the *last* thing I ever see. I may take one of them with me. But I'll be going too. I'm sure of it.

Javi makes his way in, pushing past me and noticing Chase immediately. His two cronies follow close behind him and take up positions, one in the living room and the other in the front room, with Chase capturing their full attention. The one near the hallway goes to clear the bedrooms as Javi paces the front room, one lap around with a quick glance toward Chase before he settles just in front of me.

"Take the fucking gun out of your bra and give it to me." He nods toward Chase. "Him too."

"What gun?" I ask, though I can't even rationalize why. Javi's not stupid. And he's been doing this a long time. He patiently smiles and looks over his shoulder at his minion coming back from the bedrooms. The hulking man nods and Javi nods in return.

"Gabi, Gabi, Gabi. Don't play games with me. You've worked with me for how long? Almost two years now? You know who I am. You know how I operate. Just as well as I know how you do. Now take the fucking gun out of your bra and if this puta motherfucker—" he points to Chase "—doesn't get out from behind that counter and hand over his gun, too, I'm going to shoot you both dead right where you stand. I promise you that." He puts a hand on my shoulder and I cringe. I fight the urge to put a palm into his fucking teeth and smile back instead.

"What can I do for you, Javi?"

"I told you, sweetheart. It's payday," he hisses, laughing and, thankfully, removing his hand from my shoulder and setting it to his hip. He glances over at Chase, the saccharine friendliness draining from his face and a look of resolution replacing it. Chase breathes out heavily as he slowly shuffles from behind the counter, one hand up and the other retrieving the piece from behind his back. He hands it to the goon by the hallway and stops on the other side of Javi, slipping his hands into his pockets.

Javi motions to Chase's pockets and looks him dead in the eye. "Get your fucking hands out now." Chase does and settles them onto his hips. Javi looks back at me, putting his hand up and rubbing his thumb against his ring and forefinger. "It's payday, Gabi. I *want* my fucking money."

"Javi, I told you, I don't have it all. I—"

"Give me what you got," he says, cutting me off. I nod, reluctantly slinking to my room with one of his guys following close behind, a 9 mm gripped tightly in his hand. I open a drawer and dig in, pulling out all my available cash, a wad of twenties, tens and fives I've hustled up along the way, because I know full well, he *will* see right through me if I don't grab it all. I'm just taking the quickest available route from A to B.

I walk past the beast of a man, with his fidgety finger against the trigger, and out of the room toward Javi. I hand the stack of wrinkled cash out for him and he takes it. He riffles through the bills, mumbling to himself, before folding them into a thick bundle and stuffing it into his back pocket.

"What the fuck's that?" he asks, putting another nerve-rattling hand against my shoulder. "A grand?"

"Twelve hundred," I say as Javi scans Chase. "And what do you got, pretty boy?"

I put a hand up, which Javi does not like. His head whips around and his eyes land dead on my hand.

"He's not involved, Javi," I say, lowering my arm back to my side. He lifts his hand from my shoulder and spins a forefinger in the air, his eyes scanning the ceiling and then he looks back at me.

"He's here. He's involved," Javi says, coldly, before his eyes drift back over to Chase. "Now, what do you got?"

"Honestly, all I've got is the three hundred in my wallet. That's why I'm staying here. I'm broke."

Javi laughs. "Well, well, well, looks like I'm leaving here with fifteen hundred today then, now doesn't it?" he asks.

Chase pulls his wallet out, grabs a wad of bills and hands them over. Javi takes it, pockets it, and eyes the wallet to ensure that it's empty. He nods and turns back toward me. My back is now against the wall and a hand has drifted nonchalantly to the knife tucked into my back pocket.

"You have two more weeks, Gabi," Javi says, flashing his malicious smile again as he opens the door. "Two more weeks and we kill every last one of you." He glances back at Chase before motioning for his men and heading out the door. They leave, grumbling and laughing as the door shuts behind them.

Chase looks at me, confused and just a little bit pissed off.

"Well, there's that," I say, forcing a timid smile as I slip past him and to the couch, taking a seat and burrowing my head into my shaking hands. I take deep breaths as I feel him approach and sit down on the loveseat across from me.

"And what exactly *was* that?" he asks. Pulling my face from my hands, all I can do is shake my head.

"I guess you're involved now. I should have never had you stay here. I should've known. I'm sorry for that." My head falms back into my palms and I let out a long sigh.

"Don't worry about that. It is what it is. I appreciate the place to stay. Even if it did just cost me three hundred dollars." I look up quickly, ready to give it to him good—because fuck, I just lost twelve hundred, let me lick my wounds a little first— but he has a playful smile on his face. "I'm more worried about what just fucking happened," he says, pointing to the door.

I don't say anything at first. Instead, I take a sobering breath. "A few weeks ago, I was running heroin for Javi, about twenty keys." His mouth drops, and I can almost see the judgement radiating off him. "Give me a break. It was good money and after the Army I didn't have shit."

He puts a hand up and shrugs. "Hey, no judgment here. It's just... twenty kilos... *fuck*."

"Yeah." I roll my eyes. "Judgement be damned, it's actually

not the most I've ever moved. What can I say? That spic fuck pays well." I laugh and pull a joint from my ear before offering it up.

"Fuck yeah," he says.

"Good… I'm gonna need it for this story."

The highway is vacant and dreadfully dark, but that's just how it needs to be for things such as this. Dirty deeds must be done at night, cloaked by darkness. I'm not usually this nervous, but I've got about ten kilos over what I normally roll with. That's a nice little tidbit of information Javi forgot to mention when he sent me out to Cali in this piece of shit van. The engine groans as if responding to my thoughts. I turn up the classic rock, attempting to block out the engine's complaints and these creeping, paranoid thoughts.

It doesn't work. The gram of coke I downed when I hit the Idaho state line probably didn't help much either.

Everything at night looks like a fucking cop car. With every glint of my headlights off the mile markers, my heart races and nerves spike. Mind you, I'm not scared of going to prison, my life isn't much to write home about… but I'd rather not. And twenty keys will get me put away for a real *long time. I think about the stack of hundreds waiting for me in Javi's sweaty hands when I arrive back in Trinity and I'm settled a bit, though my eyes are still peeled to the road, the speedometer reading a steady sixty-five.*

It's then two vans pull onto the highway from an on-ramp a few hundred feet ahead of me. Nothing to be alarmed about usually, as there's always a few fellow night drivers out here on these desolate roads… but two of the same type? That's what has the little hairs standing on the back of my neck. They're cruising far slower than me and as I pass them I sneak a glance as best I can through my peripherals, but can only make out a dark figure, no details. As I continue forward, my eyes are glued onto the rear-view and the four beaming headlights fading behind me.

Once they appear as just dots in the distance, my nerves relax a bit, and my focus returns to the road. I almost wish it hadn't. I wish I had looked back up and been transported to another time. To before all this recklessness and chaos. Before all the needless death.

That's not what I see though. What I see are two more identical vans pulling onto the highway from the next on-ramp. They're going considerably faster than the previous vans, and keep equal pace in both lanes. My pulse beats so loudly I can hear it throughout my head. My darting gaze shifts to the rear-view once more as the headlights come up quickly behind me now, high beams on and blinding me. I almost don't see the mess of red brake lights ahead.

I slam on my own brakes just before ramming into the back of one of them. A van behind me slams into the passenger side, spinning my vehicle into wild circles, the tires screeching below me and my brain fighting to comprehend what's just happened.

I don't have time to. After the third or fourth spin, the van rolls, flipping over the guardrail and landing hard off the road. All I can hear is crunching metal, loud violent sounds that deafen me. Through the dizziness, I see a mess of green as the grass flies by. I see glass shattering into a thousand little pieces and spraying out everywhere. I pull my arms up to block my face when the van finally settles. My head comes crashing into the driver's side window, and the lush green grass against my face fades to a sickening black. I see them approach through the blood running in my eyes, but they're just sizable figures cloaked in the darkness, guns in their hands glinting in the moon light, and haunting ski masks pulled over their heads.

"They took everything. Wallet, phone, every fucking key in the van. I ended up limping to Idaho Falls and that's when I called Shane," I say, nonchalantly, because it's no longer surreal to me. This is my life... and somehow, someway, I'm going to have to face this. "And the funny thing is, I know it was Javi. I smelled his same horrible aftershave that night."

Chase shakes his head, his hands running down each cheek. "Well, fuck. Why would he?" he asks, taking the roach from my hand, puffing it one last time before dabbing it out.

"I had turned him down a few weeks before that. He's made a few passes at me since I started working with him, but this... this was bad." I shake my head and purse my lips, my thoughts straying to the night he drunkenly made a move on me, a switchblade to my stomach, his sickening, whiskey breath hitting my neck.

"I put a knee in his balls. He was down and out after that. I thought about running, going to a different state, but he didn't remember shit the next morning. Or so I thought."

"So, why don't you run now?" Chase asks, rubbing his chin.

"Javi is part of a much larger network. And he's big time. If he wants something done... it happens. If I ran...I'd be running forever."

"And what's the alternative? Getting hacked up?"

"We're working on some things. But at the end of the day, I'm not afraid of death. Death and me," I point to my chest, "we have a real close relationship. We're fucking buddies. If it comes time for me to go, then so be it. But we'll figure something out." My eyes shift to the floor, bottom lip slipping between my teeth. I contemplate for a moment what dying at the hands of Javi would be like. It shakes me to my very core. "We have to."

CHAPTER SEVEN

Gabriela

"Machine"—Scott Helman

"JAVI CAME BY YESTERDAY," I SAY, CASUALLY, AS SHANE walks through the bedroom door, having been gone for two days, mind you. He sets his bike keys onto the vanity and takes off his jacket, tossing it to the floor.

"And?" he asks, a look of concern growing on his face. He takes a few steps forward to the end of my bed and takes a seat, his hand resting against my naked thigh. I love the wrinkle of concern he gets, just at the bridge of his nose every time he's worried about me.

I scoot closer, inadvertently moving his hand closer to my panty line. "He took everything I had. Everything that's not in the ground."

He shakes his head, his jaw clenching. "That motherfucker." He looks back at me, that adorable wrinkle between his brows again. "Did he put his hands on you?"

"No, nothing like that. I just feel like he's running out of patience." I pick at the sheets, my eyes counting their stripes. My mind wanders to sickening places, where dreadful things are done to me.

"Did he get to my shit?" he asks, leaning back and looking through the crack in the bedroom door.

"No, they didn't fuck with the drum set. They just looked around. Made some threats and made their way out," I say as my eyes settle back on his chocolate brown eyes, so full of depth and compassion.

"You have two weeks left, babe. I don't fucking get it?" He shakes his head again.

I look away in frustration. "What don't you get, Shane? He doesn't care. If he thinks I can't get it, and he knows good and well I can't get my hands on one hundred thousand, he'll just fuck with me before he eventually tortures, rapes and kills me."

Shane rears his head back, his face scrunching in disgust. "I don't fucking think so. Don't say that shit, Gabriela." He takes both my shoulders with his hands and turns me to face him. "I will never let that happen. *Never.*" His beautiful eyes are so intense, so true it makes me want to believe him. It makes me want to lie in his arms and just cry until this is all over. I want to wake up to find it's all been a sick dream. My mother would still be alive, and I wouldn't have had to watch my father slowly kill himself over the loss. There'd be no rape. No Army. No war. Everything I've ever been through would all just disappear. I'd wake up in Shane's strong arms on a beach somewhere, and we'd forget all about this ugly world.

"And how, Shane?" Tears well in my eyes because I know all too well this is not a dream. None of it has been. My reality is my nightmare… and I'm sinking fast. "How will you make sure that doesn't happen?"

He shakes me, just a little, just enough to bring my tear-coated eyes to his. He has a stern, defiant look in his eyes. "Do I know the specifics yet? No… I don't. Do I know that what I say is true… that I'll fight to the ends of the earth to protect you? Yes… yes, I do. How do I know that?" He takes one of my hands into one of his, leaving his other hand on my shoulder. He leads my hand to his chest and sets my palm against his heart. I can feel it pounding in his chest. "Because I fucking love you. I've loved you since the moment we both stood in formation as fresh fuck privates." He laughs a little and it gets one out of me, but the shake of my body sends a few tears free falling down my cheek. He takes his hand from my shoulder and runs a finger up my cheek, catching the tears and wiping them onto his shirt. I smile, appreciating so much how genuine this man is.

But he can't love me. No one can. One day, if I live through all this, he'll get sick of waiting around for me to get better and he'll find someone worth having him. Someone who can give him what he deserves.

My eyes nervously fall to the sheets again and I pull my hand away, covering myself with the comforter before reluctantly meeting his gaze. "You don't love me, Shane. You can't."

He pulls back a bit, a questioning look on his face. "And why not?"

I fight the urge to look away, lifting my chin and fighting back any tears that may want to come again. "Because I can't love you back."

He shakes his head, redirecting his attention to his jeans, he unbuttons them and slips them off.

"You may think you don't love me, gorgeous. You may have even convinced yourself of it." He turns back around to me, gripping the bottom of his v-neck with a ripped, tatted arm. With one swift motion, he removes his shirt, tossing it to the ground. He smiles, that mischievous perfect little smile of his, before sliding beneath the covers with me, his head on the pillow beside my crossed legs. I sit there, motionless, waiting for him to continue, but he initially doesn't.

He kisses my knee, keeping his lips there for a moment before pulling back. "But I know you love me," he finally says. "And I know, truer than any other words I could ever say, that I love you too."

I scoff and roll my eyes, though I know what he's saying is true. He's not looking at me anymore. His eyes are following the spinning blades of the overhead fan.

"Well then, smart guy, if you love me so damn much, where you been the past two days? I know you weren't working."

He chuckles, the evil kind of chuckle you get when someone knows something you don't.

"And how do you know that?" he asks, eyeing me curiously.

I point to the dresser where his beloved, nickel-plated Sig Sauer. "You forgot Betsy. You would've come back to get her if you had a job."

He shakes his head, laughing. "I hate you, ya know?"

"Where were you, asshole?" I ask, scrunching my eyebrows.

"Just a bit of planning," he says, his hands moving to behind his head, fingers interlocked, and a shit-eating smirk on his face.

"What kind of planning?" I raise a finger and aim it straight for him like a lecturing teacher, which draws his attention. "And you better fucking tell me."

"Listen, I may not know exactly what I'm going to do yet, but you're crazy if you think I haven't been planning. *Haven't you*?"

I put my hands up and drop them heavily to my sides. "Of course. I was SF too, Shane. I've run it around in my head a thousand times. I got nothing. So please, enlighten me."

He hesitates for a moment, garnering my best don't-fuck-around stare and he rolls his eyes. "Three different cash trucks. Three different cities. One day. All the trucks will be exactly where we need them to be at the exact time we need them to be there." His eyes drift again to the ceiling. All I can do is scoff.

"How exactly do you plan on doing that, Shane?" I ask, sarcasm thick in my tone. He ignores it.

"All I need is a driver." He nods to me. "That'd be you. I'll hit them with a roadside bomb on the highway. Nothing that'll hurt them, just a little homemade explosive to disable the vehicle and jar the driver real good. I'll hit the back door with some C4, grab the money, and you scoop me up. Then we're off to the next one." His eyes drift to the window and he looks as if he's thinking over his plan again. He smirks and nods his head, approvingly. "Yup. Cheyenne, Fort Collins, and Aspen. It's too fucking easy," he says, his eyes meeting mine again.

"Babe, please listen to what you're saying. There's an ice cube's chance in hell we pull that off on our own. There's just no way." His eyes drop, and he looks guilty for something. I've known him long enough to pick up on that. "What, Shane?"

He scratches his ear, his eyes wandering a bit before meeting mine. "I told Rock already, Gabriela. I told him the moment you told me what was going on. He's in for whatever we need."

My lips curl in disgust, nostrils flaring in a sudden surge of both embarrassment and anger. "How could you, Shane? That's the one thing I asked you not to do." I pull back, crossing my arms and shaking my head. "I cannot fucking believe you right now."

"You can't believe me?" His face changes completely, from quiet understanding to full on contempt. "Are you fucking kidding me right now, Gabriela?" He stands, snatching his clothes from the floor and putting them back on piece by piece. He retrieves his jacket and then his hat and Betsy from the dresser.

"Rock is a brother to the both of us. Of course, I'm going to fucking tell him. Besides that, have you looked at the situation you've gotten yourself into?" He points a finger at me. "Well, have you? Because if you have, you'd know that we fucking *need* him. And we need him bad."

He throws his hat on and then his jacket and opens the bedroom door. "There's one important thing to take away from this conversation. *You* got yourself into this, Gabriela. Not me. You're the one to blame for this. I told you to stay away from that shit time and time and time again." He shakes his head, a disgusted look on his face, and I can't say a word. My hands fidget in my lap and it takes everything I can to maintain eye contact. He's right, I know it, and he's the last person on this earth I want to upset.

"When you realize that I'm here for you… to support you… to do what's in your best interest always… you give me a call. Until then…" He pauses, letting out a deep sigh, and his scowl lessening. "I don't even know. I just don't know what to say anymore."

He walks out of the bedroom, closing the door behind

him, and then I hear the front door open and close as well. As his bike starts up and the growl of the motor fades down the street, I drop my head against my balled hands and cry. Wishing so much that I had the strength to chase him. To wrap my arms around his neck and tell him how much he means to me. To kiss him without regard for anything else in this world.

But I don't have the strength. I'm fresh fucking out.

CHAPTER EIGHT

Xander

"Bitter Pill"—Gavin James

THE PHONE RINGS BRIGHT AND EARLY, JARRING ME FROM my sleep. When I see Irish's name pop up on the screen through cloudy vision, I already know what's coming, and it's instantly sobering. I answer and sit up from the futon.

"What's up, man?" I ask, wiping the sleep from my eyes with my free hand.

"Good morning, budddddy," he says, a playful ring to his tone. "Really hate to bug you so early, but I got an interesting call last night from my boy Rock."

He lets an awkward pause hang on the line. I have a feeling it's far more awkward for me than it is for him.

"So, yeah, I've been meaning to call you," I say with a nervous chuckle.

"Interestingly enough, he's under the impression that I'm in Wyoming with your sister."

"What did you tell him?" I ask, my eyes shifting to the

bedroom door. My mind wondering if Gabi already knows.

"Man, first off, I think you owe me an explanation," he says, frustration building in his voice. "We're bordering on some stolen valor-type shit here that I'm not very comfortable with. I'm gonna guess your sis and her dude up there wouldn't be happy with it either."

"Listen, Irish, I'm sorry, man. I really am. I didn't know what the fuck to do. She approached me before I was ready." I pause for a brief moment. "She just caught me off guard. And I locked up. I froze. And I knew with the Rock connection, it might be an in for me. Bro… she's in some deep shit."

"I know." He lets out a sigh. "Rock inadvertently filled me in last night. And I'm down here fucking torn having been the one to send you up there, knowing it's where you need to be, while also knowing you got a woman down here who fucking needs you. She's not doing very good. Her pops is falling apart, man."

"Fuck, I don't know what to do." My head drops, my eyes close, and my mind drifts to the love of my life. The woman who steals my every thought. And how badly I wish I could be there for her.

"There's nothing you *can* do. You gotta get shit figured out up there. But do it fast. She needs you, way more than she lets on, I can promise you that."

"You trying to make me feel bad?" I ask, more defensive than I intended.

"Not at all, brother. Not one fucking bit. I'm just telling you the truth. Brandi and I are doing our best, we're doing everything we can, but we just aren't you."

A thick, choking knot sits at the base of my throat. Tears

well in my eyes and I fight with everything I have to keep them away. A few manage to escape anyway.

"I'll make a trip down soon," I finally say, wiping the tears from my cheeks with my palm.

"Okay. You do that. And bro…" His voice trails.

"Yeah?"

"Tell them the fucking truth soon. The longer you wait, the worse the repercussions are gonna be. Just be honest with her. She'll get it. Until then, don't worry about Rock. I played it off. Just make that shit happen."

"Ok. I will, man. I'm sorry again. For everything."

"Don't mention it. Just keep your head up. Shit'll work out. Shit always works out. Love ya, No homo," he says, followed by a light laugh.

"I love ya too, bro. All kinds of homo."

"Alright, talk soon."

"Peace." I hang up the phone and set it on the night stand. Shifting my legs over the side of the futon, I bury my head in my hands, hunched over my knees with my eyes tightly shut. How can I ever come out of this still standing when everyone is drowning around me? How am I supposed to be in two places at once? And how the *fuck* do I tell my sister who I really am?

Seven in the morning or not, it's time for a fucking drink.

CHAPTER NINE

Gabriela

"Monsters Calling Home"—Run River North

THE STILLNESS IN MY ROOM WITHOUT SHANE IS UNNERVING. My mind wandered all night—to him—to the years we've spent getting to know each other, supporting each other, loving each other. And yes, I do love him. I truly do. I've denied it over and over and over again over these last seven years, but the emptiness I feel right now without him is undeniable. There's just no way I'll ever tell him. No way I'll ever be able to give him what he needs.

I pull a pair of pajama pants on and control my hair behind my head in a hair tie the best I can.

Standing from the bed, I slip my feet into slippers and head to the door. Opening it, I find Chase seated on the couch and flipping through the channels. He turns to me and smiles, lifting a cup of coffee.

"Good morning!" he says, the smile still planted on his face.

"Well, aren't you just chipper this morning," I grunt, making my way to the kitchen and grabbing a cup from the cabinet. Spotting the Baileys on the counter, I turn back and smirk.

"Ahh, now I get it." I chuckle, filling my cup with both coffee and a little Baileys too. *Why the hell not?*

"I only had a few cups," he says, in the same cheerful tone.

"Sounds like you've had a little more than a few."

"I've been up awhile. Didn't sleep well last night," he says, as I take a seat on the couch across from him. He stops on ESPN and I'm thankful. I can't do the damn news. I have more than enough drama in my life.

"Yeah, me neither." I let out a heavy sigh.

"You and Shane good?" he asks, setting the remote down and taking a big sip of his coffee. He sets it to his lap, eyeing me. I take a drink of my own, my eyes drifting to the TV and then back to him.

"Don't worry about answering. It's none of my business. Just heard you guys going at it a little last night and figured I'd ask."

"No, you're fine. We're good." I grin. "It's a love-hate type of thing between us. Always has been."

"I can understand that."

"This thing... uh, with Javi..." I swallow hard, my eyes dropping to the floor. "It's not good. It's not good at all. It has him stressed."

There's a wrinkle in his brow, and he runs a jerky hand through his hair. "I know. I've been around long enough to read people. I could tell from the moment I saw that Javi guy. Even before that shit yesterday." He pauses, looking away, and as if he's pondering his next words. "What are you going to do?" he asks, a still silence sitting in the air.

"Fuck if I know," I finally respond.

"I'm going to have to go back down to Missouri soon because my g—" He stops abruptly, his face turning slightly red and he takes a thick swallow. "My wife just isn't doing well. She's got a lot going on and I need to spend some time down there…" He pauses again. "But I'll be back up to help in any way I can before it gets down to the wire."

For a moment, I don't say a thing. I can't. All I can do is wonder why the hell this perfect stranger is so willing to help. I can tell he reads the puzzlement on my face, and he just shrugs.

"I mean…you gave me a place to stay and all."

I laugh, loud and abrupt, catching both of us off guard. "Are you fucking kidding me right now? Is this like a crush thing? Are you wanting to fuck me or something? Because I don't really even know who you are. You don't know me. And these are some hard, ruthless bastards. Worst of the worst and I'm not kidding when I say that." He nods as if he actually can comprehend the capability of Javi and his crew. I've seen it with my own eyes. There are things that I've witnessed him do that haunt me worse than anything I've seen or done at war. He is an animal through and through.

"You call Rock family, right? Well, he's family to me too." He stops for a moment, taking a deep breath. "It is what it is. No need to make it a big thing."

"Alright. I guess I can live with that."

There's a long silence left in the room that's almost unbearable. A tension sits idly between us.

"You want me to find Shane?" he blurts. "Maybe talk to him. Do you know where he might be?"

"Jesus, man. You have got to be kidding me."

"Hey." He looks offended and I can't help but snicker. It's actually kinda cute. "We've hung out a lot the past week or so. We're pretty much bros now."

"So I've noticed," I say, dryly, and I roll my eyes. "Speaking of, didn't you say you came up here for work?" I ask, laughing.

"Yeah, oops," he says with a grin. "Well, I could grab a few beers with him. Or breakfast I guess." He laughs, looking at his phone and shaking his head.

"Oh no. I can guarantee you he's at the Six Shooter bull-shitting with Jimmy. If he's not here or out doing business, he's there."

My mind drifts to his plan. *Three trucks. Three cities. One Day.*

Shane was an explosives expert in the Special Forces. If anyone could pull a plan like that off, it's him. And Rock… well, Rock is just a bad motherfucker. A weapons expert with our unit, if shit went down, he's the guy we want on our side. But it's still not enough. There just aren't enough bodies. And more than likely not enough time.

"I'll head to the Six Shooter then." He finishes off his coffee and stands, heading toward the kitchen. I can only shake my head and wonder what the hell this guy's motives are.

"Whatever you say, guy. Whatever you say."

CHAPTER TEN

Xander

"The Fear"—Ben Howard

SIX BEERS DOWN AND A FUCK TON OF SMALL TALK LATER and I'm finally breaking through to him. Over the past week, we've spent a lot of time together, and I've gotten to know him a little, but Shane is a quiet man all around. He doesn't share much.

He shifts the fedora on his head, exposing the cigarette behind his ear.

"Gabriela's a complicated woman," he mumbles, following it up with a shot of Jim Beam. He grimaces and clears his throat before continuing, "She's strong." He balls his hand into a fist, shaking it a little as he looks me dead in the eye. "Strongest fucking woman I've ever known. But she's been through a hell of a lot." He drops his hand to the bar and strokes his beard with the other. "This shit though." Shaking his head, he grabs his pint glass and takes a swig of beer. "This shit's bad."

"You say she's been through a hell of a lot. Does that

include her childhood?" I ask and he eyes me curiously, which I can fully understand. It's a question I didn't give any thought to, and one that's completely ludicrous in the context of our current relationship.

"You're an odd fucking dude, Chase. An odd fucking dude." He pulls the cigarette from his ear and lights it.

"I ever tell y'all about the time my sister touched my goober?" Jimmy the bartender interrupts, much to my benefit. He's got a silly grin on his face and waits patiently for a response, as if what he's just asked isn't absolutely absurd. Shane shakes his head.

"You're fucking ridiculous, Jimmy," he says, taking a slow drag of his cigarette.

"Now hear me out, man. It was consensual." He looks at us dead serious now, and I can't help but burst out in a fit of laughter. Shane, who has obviously gotten his fill of Jimmy over the time he's been here, remains straight-faced.

"Gentlemen, I'm tryin' to have a serious conversation here. She was my first love. Have y'all ever loved before? I have. Many times. But my first love, well, that was my sister." He sets two fresh pints of beer down before us, a shit-eating grin taking up his face. He soaks up the chorus of laughter he's managed to pry out of the both of us now and shoots an air pistol at us with a click of his tongue. He then struts his way back down the bar.

"Is that guy for real?" I ask, still choking for air.

"You have no idea. He's straight out of east fucking Jesus, Alabama. He's the real fucking deal." He rolls his head to me. Making a finger gun, he pretends to shoot and then winks at me. "He's the doomsday prepper type... end of the world shit. Motherfucker's got a compound full of *all kinds* of goodies. I haven't seen it, but that's what I hear."

He takes one last drag of his cigarette before batting it out.

"Her childhood wasn't bad," Shane says out of nowhere, catching me off guard completely and eyeing me through the smoke. I keep my cool.

"Her parents, well, her adoptive parents, they were great while she was growing up. Loved the hell out of her. It's when her mom died that shit changed." He shakes his head. "She doesn't share that shit with anyone. I'm lucky."

"Fuck. What did she die of?" I ask, knowing full well that I'm pushing my luck, but risking it anyways, hoping the alcohol has helped ease him up a little, and desperately wanting to know anything and everything about this sister I've lost so much time with.

"Cancer. She was a big time smoker. They were older when they got Gabriela." He removes his fedora and sets it on the bar, running a hand through his thick brown hair. "Her dad always had a hard time with the booze and when Dotty passed... well, let's just say the tap ran freely."

He eyes his beer, a little smirk on his face and he shrugs, finishing it off and replacing it with the fresh one.

"But that's what led to the Army... And man, she loved the fucking Army. I never got into it. Hated the authority. Hated the fucking bullshit and cocky ass officers." He lifts his beer to me and nods. "Well, you know."

I chuckle and tip my beer to him, my mind racing back to the long hours I spent listening to Irish gripe about the military. I set the pint glass back to the bar. "I'm an officer myself, but I started out enlisted. I always kept that in mind."

I can't help but think of Irish and our phone call earlier. I wanted to tell the truth to Gabi right then and there, when we were sharing coffee in the living room. I just couldn't. I don't have it in me. Not yet. After I get back from Truman Valley, when I've seen Paige and I'm rejuvenated, I will be ready to tell them the truth and face this mess of a situation. Just not yet.

"I can appreciate that," Shane says. "Your type has always made the best officers." His demeanor changes, his focus locked onto the aged bar, his teeth clenching so tight I can see the ripple beneath his skin.

"Others aren't so good," he grumbles, shooting me a quick glance before averting his eyes once more.

"What's up, man? Something you wanna share?" I ask, still analyzing his expression.

"Fuck, dude," he says, finally breaking his wandering gaze and looking over at me. "If Gabriela knew I told you this, she'd probably fucking kill me. And the only reason I am telling you is because since you met Javi yesterday, you're kinda wrapped up in all this already. And because I've had three shots too many." He motions to the shot glasses turned over on the counter. "But people gotta know about this shit. It's been kept quiet for far too fucking long. The Army is always brushing it under the rug. Blaming it on the woman. 'She asked for it.' 'She just wanted a promotion.' Fuck that!" I just nod and remain silent, waiting for him to continue, but knowing full well where he's going with this. It wasn't long ago Irish told me about the terrible things that happened to my sister. Shane looks back to his beer and takes a deep breath.

"End of her last deployment in Afghanistan. I was out before that, but Rock was still in with her. They were only a few days out." He squeezes his eyes shut, his jaw clenched so tight

I can hear his teeth grinding. He clears his throat and looks at me. He doesn't just look at me, his eyes see right through me, to a different time…a different place. "A few officers gang raped her. Tricked her into opening up her door… and that was that." There's a still silence between us for a moment, his eyes straight ahead before he finally looks back over at me. "I should've been there."

He scoffs, lighting up another cigarette and squeezing the filter mercilessly between two fingers. I don't dare talk. I just wait for him to continue. "And the motherfuckers got off. There wasn't enough evidence. There wasn't fucking any. And her commander was the cock sucking ring leader. Nothing. She got out. They retired on some fat fucking pensions. Some of them are still leading troops in battle."

"Jesus. You gotta be fucking kidding me," I mutter, my mind racing to all the things Gabi must be feeling right now… what she's been feeling for years. I knew she had been raped, but this? I just can't even imagine. We've been apart for so long and somehow this cold world has distributed both of us our fair share of pain and suffering. A throbbing tightness buries itself in my heart and I'm hit with an intense desire to tell her, to find the strength somehow, so that I could hold her and let her know I'd be there for her no matter what. That I always will be.

"I wish I was. But I'm not. It happened. And it fucking ruined her." He pauses, his eyes drifting to Jimmy, who quickly makes his way toward us. It looks as if he's fighting back tears.

"There's so much dick in here I feel like I'm hanging out in Kim Kardashian's asshole. Ya know what I mean?" Jimmy says, two more cold beers in his hands.

"Jimmy, you have terrible timing," Shane says, shaking his

head and slipping his Ray-Bans on.

Jimmy pulls the beers to his side and looks offended. "That's not what your empty fuckin' beer is saying," he grunts and nods to the empty pint glass in front of Shane. He rolls his eyes and sets the fresh beers down. A nauseating tightness takes hold in my stomach. I've had way too much beer already before noon.

Jimmy remains standing in front of us, a hand to his gut and a curious look on his face.

"Y'all ever seen midgets run track?" He smiles, a twinkle in his eye that one can't help but grin at. "That shit's funny as fuck." He pauses, his focus drifting to the ceiling as if he's recalling a past memory. "I had a cousin who fucked a midget once. Said that shit was tighter than an Amish sheep's asshole, but her heels kept banging into his stomach like a fuckin' drum. Bruised him up real good."

And with that, he makes his way back down the bar, whistling away as if the shit he just spewed were as normal as hello.

Shane lets out a deep breath, grabbing his hat from the bar and putting it back on his head. He digs into his back pocket and pulls out a wallet. Flipping through it, he grabs two twenties and tosses them on the bar.

"I'm not trying to drink another beer. Jimmy will finish these, I can promise you that." He turns to me, standing from his stool and pocketing his wallet. "You wanna go grab some chow?"

A feeling of relief washes over me, my stomach immediately craving anything that's not alcohol as I finish the remainder of my beer. I set it on the bar and stand along with him.

"Fuck... yes."

As we hit the door, he props a forearm against it, but doesn't push it open. He turns to me, eyeing me curiously. "Enlisted *and* an officer? How the fuck old are you? You look about twelve."

I let out a nervous laugh as he swings the door open and walks out. "Yeah, I get that a lot."

———————————————

Playing along with my assumed role, I've spent a few days away from Trinity 'looking for wood' as I told Shane and Gabi before leaving. In reality, I've been staying in a drab motel room in the middle of nowhere, and bored out of my ever-loving mind. Time is a funny thing when you're isolated and struggling. Minutes and hours run together, and your mind starts playing tricks on you. You hear things. You see things. And you think about damn near every problem you've ever had.

As I lay in the stiff motel bed, cloaked in darkness with only the little red alarm clock numbers to keep me company, my thoughts stray to Paige. It's been nearly an hour since I said good night to her and the tone in her voice is still very clear in my head. She's getting worse… detached and withdrawn. She's losing herself a little more each day and it kills me to know I should be there. After figuring out this shit with Gabi, I have every intention of heading down to Truman Valley to spend a few days with Paige, but that certainly doesn't help me me to sleep tonight .

My eyes are wide open, my heart beating relentlessly in my chest, and the guilt is like a vice against my throat. Not since deciding to confess to Teresa's murder have I been so goddamn torn. What would I do if Paige lost the will to go on? What if it happened while I was away? The thought of it alone brings me so much anguish that tears form in my eyes, and an ache strangles my heart.

I reach a hand out and snag my cell from the nightstand. Pulling up my photo album, I swipe through the only pictures I've taken since getting out of prison, five in all, and each one of Paige and me. The tears fall freely now as the pain of missing her numbs my body.

What if she doesn't make it through?

Abruptly, the phone rings loudly in my hand, her name flashes on the screen, and a sickening feeling takes hold in my gut.

CHAPTER ELEVEN

Paige

Present

"Poison & Wine"—The Civil Wars

I KNOW MY LIFE HASN'T ALWAYS BEEN THIS WAY. I KNOW ONCE not long ago I had a loving family. I knew no such thing as fear back then, and hate, and rage. I knew nothing of the ache that's taken hold of my insides, twisting and turning them in a constant upheaval. I never thought my life would turn out this way, but now that it has, I can hardly remember the life I led before it. It fades quickly, drowned out in tears, picked apart piece by piece from guilt.

I'm drained of everything.

Brandi holds me, like she's been holding me since I ran from my car into her arms the night it happened… since I found *him.* I cried out for her, for my best friend in this world, without regard as to who could hear me. She pulled me inside, though my legs were numb and fighting against her. I tried to walk. I just couldn't. Finally, Chase had to bucket carry me into the living room, my snotty nose nuzzling into his shoulder. And here I've been since, crying and thinking, then crying some more.

What the hell do I do now? Where do I go from here?

"Babe, can I get you anything? Anything at all?" Brandi asks, giving me a good squeeze. I face her, my eyes red and achy, but the ugliness of it concealed by the dark room. I'm wrapped in the blankets, wishing so much that it was Xander's arms.

"I'm okay," I murmur and force a weak smile. She gives me another good squeeze before releasing me and scooting off the bed and onto her feet. As she heads toward the door, the rip of a motorcycle engine grows in intensity. She turns back toward me, her mouth agape. Eyes wide, I turn back and catch a single headlight coming from the long driveway. I look back at Brandi, shaking my head in disbelief and the tears begin streaming down my face.

"Oh, my God!" Brandi squeals, pulling her hands to her mouth. "He's here." She grabs me by the arm and pulls me up, but she doesn't have to. I'm on my feet and out the door faster than I can even process a thought.

I hear the engine cut off just as I reach the front door, turn the handle and pull it open.

He's still straddling the Harley as he pulls his helmet off. There's a tired, but excited look in his eye. He throws the helmet to the dirt, climbs off the bike and I run to him, my feet moving outside of my control, driven by a need to be in his arms. He grabs me, pulls me in, and kisses me so hard my entire body quivers. He grips my thighs and pulls my legs up and around his waist. I lock my feet together, and I stare deep in his eyes.

"I've missed you so, so much," he says, his eyes beginning

to glisten over.

I don't say a word because I can't even gather my thoughts. I just know I need his lips on mine. I need to feel him, all of him, and all of his love. I need to feel anything but this retched pain. I need to be taken away. Bringing my lips to his ear, I take a heavy breath in, my heart pounding in my chest.

"Take me to my room," I whisper. "Take me there now, baby."

He sets me down lightly on the bed, having carried me through the house, my head nuzzled into his shoulder, the tears running freely.

"Baby?" he whispers softly against my mouth. "I don't even know what to say." His bottom lip slips between his teeth, his eyes full of concern. "I want so much to—" I cut him off with a finger to his lips.

"You don't need to say anything right now, baby. Just take me. Make me forget all of this. Please?" I grab a fistful of his hair and pull him into me, kissing him hard, my lips crashing and cascading against his. I need him. I need all of him. I use my other hand to grip his wife beater and I tug it up and over his head, his arms high in the air to help me.

He comes down, his lips against my neck and he gives me light nibbles as he pulls my shorts and already wet panties off in one swift movement. His body charges back into mine and the feeling of his growing cock against my entrance shoots chills up my spine. He pulls the shirt over my head and brings his lips down on my left nipple, sucking and tugging it lightly with his teeth, and it stiffens immediately inside his mouth, begging for more.

I grab aimlessly at his pants, my hands not quite working

with the button on his jeans, but it's enough to get my point across. He scatters kisses down my stomach, unbuttoning his jeans and pushing them down to his knees just as his breath finds my clit. My body arches, craving him to take me… every bit of me. He kicks off his jeans and looks at me, a fire in his eyes, and then directs his attention back to my pussy, admiring it, then possessing it. His tongue licks and circles around my swollen bud, causing my legs to tremble.

"Oh, my God, right there. Right fucking there, Xander," I say in a breathy gasp.

"You taste so fucking good, baby." He shakes his head. "So fucking good." With that, he buries his face again, causing my body to go into uncontrollable spasms. My toes curl, the muscles flexing and cramping. This is what I want. This is what I *need*.

"Fuck, baby. I need you inside me, right now!" I moan, grabbing at his thick arms. "Please, fuck me." He gives me one more delicate lick and then brings his lips to mine. I can taste myself on him and it fills me with a complete desire to have his thickness inside of me.

He stares deep into my eyes, both sorrow and lust filling them. "I love you, Paige. I love you so much," he says, kissing my forehead.

"I love you too, Xander. Now, take me. Fucking take me."

The tip of his dick meets my entrance and he settles it there for a moment before teasing me inch by inch as he slowly glides inside me. I let out a whimper, an ache taking hold inside of me equal parts pain and pleasure.

"Yes. *Yes.*" I hardly recognize my own voice. The words come out on their own free will. "God, yes. Fuck me, Xander.

Fuck me."

He picks up speed, his girth making my body seize with pleasure. He takes a soft bite into my neck, his hot breath forced in and out against my skin as he continues pumping, faster and faster and faster. He moans, releasing my neck and kissing me with everything he has. I can feel the love pass between us like an electrical current. He needs me just as much as I need him. I can feel it in the way he handles me, the way he stares deep into my eyes as our bodies connect and become one. Wrapped in his perfect arms is where I'm meant to be, and it's the only thing that can take this pain in my heart away, or at least numb it for a little while. I can't be away from him again, that much I know. It will be the death of me. He's the only thing I have left. He is my safe haven, his arms protection against the vile outside world.

He quietly holds me, thinking I'm still sleeping, our first morning waking up next to each other in weeks. It feels all too perfect. And it reinforces the idea that being without him again is an impossibility. I won't let it happen again.

I feel his lips meet my forehead before he rustles from under the covers and stands. I open my eyes and watch him as he moves across the room.

"Hey, where you going? Leaving me already?" I ask, rubbing the sleep from my eyes.

He turns and smiles. "Morning, sleepyhead. I was just going to grab some coffee. You want some?"

"Yeah, I'll come with." I toss the blanket aside and meet him by the door.

We make our way to the kitchen, hand in hand, and find Chase and Brandi already seated at the kitchen table with half eaten breakfast in front of them.

"Morning, you two," Chase says, giving me a wink. "Didn't get much sleep, huh?" He laughs as I reach into the cupboard for two coffee mugs. Xander grabs the Baileys from the fridge with a smirk.

"Can you blame me?" Xander asks grabbing a handful of my butt. I look back at him with a smile and he kisses me on the cheek. We take a seat with our coffees and Chase just shakes his head.

"Not one bit," he says with a smirk. "How the hell'd you manage to drive all that way in one sitting? How far was it anyways? Twenty hours?"

"About that," Xander says with a laugh. "It was something like twenty-one with stops and all." He looks to me, sincerity in his eyes, and takes the nape of my neck in his hand, softly squeezing. "But how could I not." He looks back at Chase, the smile still on his face and says, "She's worth every damn mile."

Brandi awwwwws and Chase just chuckles and shakes his head.

"You're the man, Xander," he says, knowing full well Xander is exactly what I needed after the awful two days I've had since Dad's passing. And with his funeral two days from now... I don't even know how I'll handle it. "How are things up in Wyoming by the way? Things all cleared up?" Chase asks with an eyebrow raised. Xander's eyes shift down to the table-top as he picks at his fingernails.

"About the same, man. Sorry. This was all..." He looks at me, remorse in his eyes. The same remorse that's been there since he drove up last night. "It was just out of nowhere. I didn't have the chance to." Chase looks annoyed but nods his head.

"When you get back then? The truth?" he asks.

"The truth, I promise. Right when I get back," Xander says, and without thought I take his hand into mine.

"I'm going with you," I blurt out as tears begin to creep up. "I can't stay here."

"Babe, there's nothing I want more than for you to come with me, but it's looking ugly up there. I just don't know if I want you involved," he says, sincerity in his words. He only wants what's best for me. I know that, but nothing is going to keep me away from him again. Nothing is going to keep me in Truman Valley.

"I don't give a shit, Xander. I'm coming. I can't stay here," I plead, tears beginning to run down my cheeks now in full force.

"We're all coming with you, brother," Chase says, taking my other hand into his and squeezing it. "Right after the funeral."

"And who made that decision?" Xander asks, removing his hand from mine and shaking his head. "Was anyone going to ask me what I thought about it?"

"No, we weren't," Chase says in a matter of fact tone. "We love you, bro. And as such, we're going to have your back in this. That's all there is to it."

Xander stands abruptly, pushing the chair back with a loud screech. He goes to say something but doesn't, shaking his head instead and walking back to my room.

"Xander!" Chase calls out, but he continues to the room anyways. I put my hand up, stopping Chase from following Xander, and I stand myself.

"I got it," I say, heading down the hall and into my room

where Xander sits on my bed with his head in his hands.

"Baby, I can't stay here," I say, the tears starting to return. "I just can't. Everywhere I look I think of them. Everything I see in this fucking town reminds me of them. I just can't do it anymore. I just can't!" I cry out, dropping to my knees. This isn't how I wanted to handle the situation, but my emotions are out of control right now, my grief insurmountable.

Xander quickly makes his way off the bed and kneels down next to me, wrapping his arms around me.

"Okay, baby. Okay. I'm sorry," he whispers. "I'm so sorry."

"I know…you only want…what's best for me," I squeak out between sobs. "But what's best for me… is to be with you. You're the only thing I have left." The tears seep into his shirt turning red to crimson. "You're all I have," I repeat, snorting and sniffling through the current bout of tears.

"I'm here, Paige. I'm here. I'll never leave your side again. I promise you." He takes me in a tight embrace and kisses my forehead, letting his warm lips stay right there, right where I ache for them to be.

CHAPTER TWELVE

Xander

"Young Bodies"—Westward the Tide

THERE WERE TIMES DURING THE FUNERAL I WASN'T SURE Paige was going to make it. I feel as if I watched her heart get ripped from her chest over and over again. I thank God it was a closed casket. I don't think she would've been able to stay as strong otherwise. I don't know how she's even staying as strong as she is. I can only imagine she's stuffing it deep down, to simmer and boil beneath the surface before one day it's unleashed onto her. And I will be there for her, but I fear the day it comes. I fear what it will do to her.

She clings to my back tightly as the Harley rips down the rural South Dakota highway, wheat flowing in the wind like waves crashing against the roadside shore as the sun begins its descent into the horizon. Brandi leads the pack in a loaded-up SUV, Rowdy along for the ride with his snout out the window, and Irish is just behind her on his own hog. Paige settles her helmeted head against my shoulder, giving me a good squeeze, just as the SUV's turn signal flashes on.

We stop at a rundown gas station just off the highway. An old man in overalls seated on the bench tips his trucker's hat as we pull up alongside each pump. The old ice machine grunts and grinds in the still country silence. Irish pulls his helmet off and lifts his leg up and over the bike. I do the same, letting Paige dismount first, and Brandi meets the three of us by the pump.

"I'm thinking we fuel up here and maybe call it a night. We can finish out the final leg in the morning. What do ya think?" Irish asks, wiping a gloved hand over his sweaty forehead.

"I'm fine with it," I say, glancing around our vicinity, only a McDonald's and a wretched-looking motor lodge in view. "But here?"

Irish laughs and shakes his head. "Not unless you're trying to catch something," he jokes.

"Yeah, I don't think so..." Brandi says, her lip curled in disgust. "Not a chance in hell. I just gotta tinkle." She throws a thumb back toward the convenience store and then motions for Paige. "You coming, boo?"

"Good luck with that, ladies," I say, peering off at what looks to be an outhouse. "Maybe bring a weapon."

Brandi laughs, patting a hand against her waistband. "Never leave home without it." She winks, looping her arm around Paige's and they head toward the *Wrong Turn*-like porta-potty.

"I taught my girl well," Irish says with a smirk, before making his way to the pump to fuel up.

"You ever get ahold of Gabi by the way?" he asks as I begin fueling up my own ride.

"I sent another text about three hours ago, and called to

leave a message this morning," I say. The thought of what's to come like a dense fog in my brain, overshadowing all else. I'll have to tell her. I have no other choice as Irish is now coming with me. I know it's the right time, even if it seems far too late. I just keep thinking about how completely ridiculous this conversation will be, and my brain runs around in circles as to what type of response I'll receive.

"You mention anything?" he asks, an eyebrow arched.

"No, man, I told you, I can't do that over text. I'll pull her aside when we first get there. I just wish she'd get back to me. No idea what's going on," I say, concern washing over me. Visions of life draining from her eyes taking hold.

"She's alright, brother. Positive thinking," Irish says.

"Yeah." Scoffing, I put the pump nozzle back in its place as the girls approach. "That glass half full shit… I fucking *hate* that."

We pull up to Gabi's house after nearly seven hours on the road. My back is stiff and achy, but that's not what's on my mind. Having heard back from Gabi late last night, I at least know she's okay, but that doesn't take away from the fact that I have a heavy conversation to take on here in a few minutes and it's not something I'm even remotely ready for. There's a new bike in the driveway, one I haven't seen, and an uncomfortable feeling washes over me.

Paige, Irish and I dismount the bikes as Brandi exits the SUV, stretching her arms out wide into the air with a loud sigh as Rowdy hops out behind her, running to the side yard to relieve himself. The swing of the front door pulls my eyes from Paige to Gabi as she and Shane walk down the porch steps, beers in hand.

"You weren't kidding. You brought an army with you," Gabi says, taking a seat on the last porch step. She tokes on a joint pinched between two fingers.

"Yeah, sorry, we aren't trying to stay or anything. Just dropping by for a quick hello," I say, my heart beating hard in my chest.

"Oh, I don't care. I told you that last night. We can have a damn pow wow," she says, the smoke wafting around her head. Paige takes two steps forward with her hand out.

"Hey, I'm Paige. Xander's girlfriend," she says and the sound of my actual name leaving her lips stills my heart. She still doesn't realize what she's said when Gabi gets up and takes her hand, shaking it before offering up the joint.

"Wanna hit?" Gabi asks, and Paige eagerly takes it from her. Gabi nods toward Irish. "That must make you Xander?" she asks him and he looks over at me, worry and confusion written on his face, before his eyes fall back on her.

"Uhhh." It's all he can manage. It doesn't matter anyways. Through the door comes a tanned, pit bull-looking dude with a military crew cut. His tattooed hands tighten his belt buckle. I don't know who he is, but the memorial band on his wrist and haircut lets me know it's probably not good for me.

As his head raises and he catches sight of Irish, I know for a fact it's not good for me. His eyes light up and he scurries down the steps, his shredded arms wide open.

"Irish fuckin' McGregor! You big ugly fuck!" He embraces Irish, who embraces him back, but his wide eyes bounce from me, to Gabi and Shane who now look utterly confused, heads tilted and brows scrunched. "Shit, it's damn good to see ya," the man says in his thick country twang.

"It's great to see you too, Rock," Irish says, as he slaps hands with who I now know is the legendary Rock Callahan... and that I am completely *fucked*.

"Uhhh, Chase, what's going on?" Gabi asks me, drawing the attention of Rock. His eyebrow arches as he analyzes me.

"Gabs, what are ya talkin' about?" He points to Irish. "This is Chase. I don't know who *that* is." He motions to me.

"Gabi, can we speak in private," I say in an almost whisper.

"No. You've got some explaining to do to all of us it seems," she says, her hands meeting her hips.

Paige wanders back over to me and puts an arm around me, squeezing my waist. "I'm sorry," she whispers.

"Please, Gabi. Just a little privacy first. I'll explain everything," I say, looking her in the eyes now. She's livid, her head turning from side to side.

"Who the fuck are you?" she asks. Shane slips a finger in her back pocket and pulls her back toward him. His eyes are on me... studying me.

"Listen, Gabriela...er Gabi...I'm Chase McGregor. I went to basic with Rock. This is my wife, Brandi," Irish says, motioning for Brandi who puts a reluctant hand out for Gabi but gets no response. Gabi's raging eyes are still on me... still hungry for answers. Irish motions toward me. "This is one of my best friends in the world, Xander, and I'm begging you to give him a few minutes in private and let him explain..." He puts his hands together. "*Please.*"

Gabi looks at him, her angry eyes remaining there for

a moment before they come back to mine. "Fine," she says. "You've got two minutes." She turns and heads up the steps. Without turning around, she adds, "*c'mon.*"

She paces the front room, waiting for me to come through the door. When I do, she meets me in the foyer, a deep furrow in her brow. "Speak," she barks, pointing a finger at me.

"Gabi..." My eyes drift to the living room and then back to her. "Can we sit down or something?"

"No, we can't. You've been pretending to be someone else. Staying in my damn house. You need to talk and you need to talk right goddamn here...right goddamn now." Her jaw clenches, hands balling into tight fists.

"Shit..." I shake my head, eyes lowering to the floor and I run a slow hand through my hair. I take a thick dry swallow, the words just a jumbled mess in my brain.

How the fuck do I do this?

"I just don't even know where to start..." My voice trails.

"Start from the fucking beginning," she says, a bite to her words and I can't help but let out a nervous chuckle.

"It's funny you say that. Do you remember your birth parents? Anything at all?" I ask.

She pulls back, her face scrunched in confusion. "How in the hell is that any of your business? And how the hell did you know I was adopted?" Her eyes shoot past me and to the front door. "It was Shane, wasn't it? That prick, I'm gonna beat his ass," she snarls, her angry eyes settling back on me.

"Listen..." I swallow hard and clear my throat. "Have you ever checked into your past? Found anything out about your birth parents?" I ask and she shakes her head, her anger turning to complete confusion.

"What are you getting at, Chas…" she cuts herself off, then continues, "…or whatever the fuck your name is."

"Xander… my name is Xander Evans, and I'm your brother. Your birth parents are Robert and Grace Evans."

Her mouth falls open and she jerks her head back. "What the fuck are you talking about?"

CHAPTER THIRTEEN

Gabriela

"Digging Shelters"—Neil Halstead

"My name is Xander Evans... and I'm your big brother," he repeats, but the words just don't seem real to me.

"Are you fucking with me here?" I ask, unable to come up with anything else to say.

He darts his eyes around the room, biting his lower lip before he finally looks back at me again. "Your parents died from a murder suicide." He pauses, taking a deep breath. "Our parents."

My thoughts racing, I manage my way to the living room and take a seat on the edge of the couch, burying my head in my hands as panic grips my chest.

"This can't be fucking real," I mutter into my hands as I feel him move closer.

"It's real, Gabi. And I'm sorry you had to find out this way. I wanted to tell you..." his voice trails off.

"So why didn't you?" My voice raises more than intended.

"I mean, think about it. How exactly does one go about that?" he asks followed by a light chuckle. I lift my head from my hands, an eyebrow raised, anything but amused.

"I don't know... say something for Christ's sake. Don't pretend to be your friend. And then stay in my damn house."

"I know, I know... but for real." He puts his hand out and plants a shit-eating grin on his face. "Am I supposed to be like 'Hey, little sis, long lost big brother here! How ya doing?'" He gives a goofy thumbs up for good measure and it earns him a laugh, though I stifle it quickly.

"Alright, but fuck. This is some heavy shit," I say, rubbing my temples.

"You're telling me. It's kind of ridiculous."

I stand, fumbling with my pockets for no good reason and the awkwardness in the room making me uneasy. I feel like this man I've known for two weeks is a complete stranger.

"Can we hit up Six Shooter maybe? All of us? I need some liquor to have this conversation."

"I second that," he says, laughing.

<hr />

Paige, Brandi and I make it in the bar first, sharing some uneasy small talk. The guys remain outside, smoking a joint and working out what exactly just went down. As we post up at the empty bar, Jimmy curls a finger for me to come over and I reluctantly do, leaning in as the other two take up two stools at the bar.

"Well now, darlin', what did you bring me here?" he asks, nodding toward Brandi who is mid discussion about drink orders with Paige and doesn't notice. "Now, I'd baste that butthole and eat it for Thanksgiving dinner," he says, licking his lips and then purring, batting a hand as if it were a paw.

"Even if she weren't taken, Jimmy, you'd have an ice cube's chance in hell," I say, rolling my eyes. "Grab two beers for me and Shane. Not sure about everyone else."

Jimmy's eyes are still on Brandi and he winks at the back of her head. "I got something for her to drink."

"Hey, Jimmy, stop jerking around and get me a beer already."

He side eyes me and puts a hand to his hip. "You know, if your father wasn't such a good friend to me, I'd likely bend you over my knee."

"You'd like that too much," I crack, greeting Shane who approaches from behind me with a kiss to my cheek. He waits for me to sit and offers up the stool on my left to Xander, who takes the seat with a nod of appreciation. Shane sits on my right and Rock takes up a stool next to him, though his attention is locked on a group in the back who are playing pool and heckling each other loudly. Who I now know to be the real Chase takes a seat on the far side of the ladies. It's probably the first time in this bar's existence that every stool is occupied.

As Jimmy puts beers down for me and Shane, Xander motions for one of his own, and Jimmy then makes his way to the others. I nervously sip my beer, my foot bobbing relentlessly. Right about now I could go for some coke. Of course, I'm dry, and my guy is dry, so I'm left to tend to this situation with some liquor anesthetics instead.

Shane must notice my inner turmoil because he slips a hand to my bobbing knee, giving it two good squeezes before he kisses me softly on the cheek. His lips move to my ear and he whispers, "I'll give you guys some time. Gonna go play some better music." He kisses me again and starts toward the jukebox by the pool table.

Noticing Shane's departure, Rock leans in, grabbing his Long Island and sweeping a tanned hand over the top of his head, he says, "I'm gonna make some rounds. I wanna get me some Wyoming booty."

Xander looks around curiously, before turning back to Rock with a chuckle. "Ummm, I'm not sure if you see what I see, but I think women avoid this place."

Rock laughs, standing, and he pats Xander on the back. "Oh, that's quite alright with me." He winks and clicks his tongue before following Shane to the jukebox.

Xander shakes his head. "I did not see that coming." He looks around again, analyzing the flannelled clientele scattered throughout the room. His eyes trail back to me and he cracks a smile. "I'll tell you what though, he'd probably have better luck if he were straight."

I laugh and take a swig of beer. "Don't underestimate my guy. I've seen him make moves in far more bigoted places than here. He's a pro at picking out the weak ones."

"You make it sound like it's a Discovery channel show," Xander cracks.

"For Rock, that's about how it is. Fucking and fucking people up. The two things he's best at," I say, thinking back on the numerous times I've seen Rock beat the ever-loving shit out of some mouthy homophobe. It's one of my favorite things to witness.

"I think you mentioned something before about him

working in Vegas?" he asks.

"Yeah, he works for some not so good people doing some not so good things. He's pretty much a fixer for the casino underbelly."

Xander just laughs and shakes his head.

"What?" I ask, eyeing him.

"Nothing," he says, smiling against his beer bottle.

"None of this 'nothing' bullshit. Speak."

He tilts his head to me, his eyes up and mouth half open as if in mid thought. "I guess…" He pauses and clears his throat. "I've known a lot of veterans in my lifetime. They're all incredible human beings… but you guys tend to mess around with some crazy shit."

"Well, I'm not denying it, but what do you mean?" I ask.

"Hmmm, like Rock with the Vegas business, my boy Irish racing illegally, I have this friend Twitch, my old cell mate, and he got caught up living on the edge too. And then you and…" his voice trails as his eyes fall to the bar. "Just with all that stuff."

"Yeah, I hear you. There are a lot of us. Uncle Sam's misguided children they call us. I think we just get out, after fighting and adrenaline-charged living, and, I don't know…" I shake my head, knowing it's a multitude of reasons we are the way we are. Far too many to list. "I think it's partly for the adrenaline rush… maybe a little boredom… definitely a good deal of carelessness mixed in there."

"Do you miss it," he asks, and immediately I'm torn.

"At times… yeah," I say, nodding. "But I went through a lot with them at the end there. No matter what good I can recall about my Army career. It'll always be overshadowed by that shit."

"Sorry to bring it up. I'm sure it's a touchy subject."

I laugh, grabbing and polishing it off. "Considering the situation, I'd say we're okay. Speaking of touchy subjects... prison?" I ask, scrunching my brow.

He takes a thick swallow, nervously picking at his beer label. "Yeah, that's quite the story. Long story short, I was falsely convicted. Spent three-plus years in a Missouri state prison."

"Oh wow... how long have you been out?"

He laughs with a quick shake of his head. "A little over a month," he says.

I pull my head back, a look of disbelief on my face.

"Wait, what?! Then what the hell are you doing here?"

He looks at me as if I'm stupid. "For you, Gabi."

"What do you mean 'for me'? If you just got out of prison you don't need to be getting caught up in my shit."

"Like it or not, Gabi, you're my sister... and I'm your older brother. And you're all the family I've got. No matter how much time it's been, I'll never forget the two years I spent with you," he says, his eyes drifting along the bar top.

"You really remember back then?"

"I do. I'll never forget it." His eyes meet mine and they're full of sadness.

"What do you remember?" I ask, curious about my childhood as everything before four is blocked out... everything before my adoptive parents took me.

"I remember despite our surroundings, you were the happiest little baby. We used to lie on the floor together, on 'our' blanky and the TV would play whatever daytime television garbage was on. We were soap opera veterans at a very young age," he says, laughing.

"Were they ever happy? Our biologicals."

Lines form in his forehead as he looks out along the top shelf.

"You know," he says, looking back over at me. "My brain blocked a lot out… but from what I do remember… no. They never were. It was…" his voice trails as he scratches his five o'clock shadow. "It was just bad," he continues. "I'm just glad you found a loving family."

"Were you ever adopted?" I ask, and I notice his jaw tenses up. He takes a swig of beer and gives a quick shake of his head.

"Nah."

"I'm sorry, Xander." I swallow, trying to push past the uneasy lump in my throat. I never imagined being in this position before. *Never.*

His eyes dart to me and he shakes his head. "No, don't apologize. I'm happy as hell you were adopted. We were probably going to be separated regardless."

"I love my parents. They were amazing for the most part… but I wish we had some sort of family that could've taken us in. Maybe things could've been different."

"Maybe," he says, nodding. "Maybe not. My life's not a sitcom by any means. It's been ugly. And miserable. And ruthless at times. But at the end of the day, I'm with a woman I love, I'm drinking ice cold beer, and I'm catching up with a sister who I haven't seen in twenty-five or so years." He tips his beer to me. "And there's something to be said for that."

I click my beer against his and smile, taking a slow sip as a silence sits between us for a moment.

"What brought you back here anyways?" he asks, looking around and laughing. "I mean, why *here*?"

"Well, you know, I got out of the Army and I was lost. When Dad was going through the worst of it I had to come back for that anyway. It felt like it was the right thing to do. And then, after the Army I missed the brotherhood... the camaraderie. My dumb ass thought a gang might satisfy that feeling." I shrug.

"About the Army..." he says, his voice trailing as he rubs a finger and thumb in his eyes. "I have to admit something."

CHAPTER FOURTEEN

Xander

"Wildfire"—Mandolin Orange

"F UCK, THIS ISN'T EASY." MY EYES FALL TO THE BAR AS I mindlessly tap a thumb against it. "I know about what happened to you in the Army. While I was in prison, the real Chase kept tabs on you through Rock. He told me about what happened before you got out. He told me about everything. That's why I came. I just want you to know. I'm here for you if you need *anything*."

She doesn't speak for a moment, simply staring at the beer clutched in her hand. The silence runs my thoughts rampant.

"I know it's not the same thing..." I continue, anything to snuff this terrible silence. "But I went through similar things in foster care." I take a thick swallow as I feel her eyes finally drift to me. I don't look at her though. I can't. The very few times I've talked about this kind of thing to people in my life I've felt the judgment come off them in waves. It's why I keep it so buried.

"I'm sorry I got adopted and you didn't. It wasn't right for them to separate us," she finally says, drawing my eyes to her.

"Don't even. I'm glad you could have some sort of normalcy growing up. Seriously. We may not know much about each other, but there hasn't been a day that's passed where I haven't thought about you and hoped for the best."

She flashes a timid smile before waving Jimmy down.

"Any more of this deep shit and I'm gonna need a few shots," she cracks as Jimmy approaches from the other end of the bar.

"What can I get ya, darlin'?" he asks. "Besides my ten-inch pecker."

Gabi laughs. "Ten inches, huh? Jimmy, you looking at yourself in a funhouse mirror or something? I know you've got a baby dick in those jeans, so don't go kidding either one of us and grab me some damn shots already."

"Well shit, Gabi. Don't go dirty talkin' to me just to send me away with a pair of blue balls," Jimmy says, wiggling his brows.

"Five shots of Fireball or I detach the blue balls from your body," she says, glancing down the bar at Irish, Brandi and Paige. "You guys want a shot, right?" They nod and she looks back at Jimmy. "And why don't you grab one for yourself, Jimbo."

He meanders away, mumbling under his breath, but shooting a quick smile toward Gabi before grabbing a handful of shot glasses.

"I honestly don't know how the hell I got back here," Gabi says abruptly. She looks around the bar and shakes her head.

"Outside of the Army, this place is all I ever knew," she continues. "Once Dad passed, I just didn't know where else to go. The Army was my life for a long time. I was a fucking wreck without it. I still am."

"I can only imagine."

There's a comfortable silence that sits between us as we watch Jimmy pour the shots in front of us. He's grinning back at us like an idiot.

"What, no shot for me?" Rock calls from behind us and I look back to see a wide smile on his face.

"I thought you'd be dick deep inside a country boy, Rock. My fault," Gabi says and he doubles over in laughter.

"What, no luck?" I ask, a smirk on my face.

Once Rock contains himself and straightens, he holds up a book of matches between two fingers. It has a name and number written in pen on the flap. "Think again, new guy," Rock says, pursing his lips. "Later tonight that ass is mine."

"Well, I'll be damned," I say, eyeing the matchbook as he pockets it.

"I'm telling you," Shane says, coming up from behind Rock and throwing an arm around his neck. "My boy's got mad game. Now grab me one of those too, Jimmy."

Jimmy pours two more shots and then lines the bar with them. Each of us takes a shot glass but our eyes wander, waiting for someone else to lead the cheers.

"Shit, I'll get it then," Jimmy says, clearing his throat. "Here's to those who sit when they pee. We love 'em in leather. We love 'em in lace. But we love 'em the best when they sit on our face." A smattering of 'here-heres' and laughter precedes eight shots downed between us and the thump of all the shot glasses hitting the bar top.

"Fuck, I love that shit," I say, a burn tearing down my throat.

Jimmy leans in to Gabi and whispers, "Now, I hate to do this because you know I love y'all coming up and seeing me. But word is 'you know who' will be up here tonight. And soon. Might be best for y'all to continue the party elsewhere."

Gabi nods in appreciation. "Thanks, Jimmy. Why don't you get us another round of shots and the check?"

"You got it, darlin'."

Her focus trails back to me and she must catch the concern in my eyes because she looks away quickly.

"What are you going to do about that? What can you do?" I ask.

"Shit. Your guess is as good as mine. I need money. A lot of it… And fast." She shrugs, swigging the last of her beer. "It's all just shit."

Once the last round of shots is downed and the tab is paid, we bid farewell to Jimmy and make our way outside. As we pass through the doors and straddle our respective motorcycles, the growl of incoming engines and bright headlights pulls our attention. I start up my own bike and Paige hops on behind me as Javi and his crew pull up. They dismount their bikes and walk slowly to the front door, their attention on Gabi. One of his crew opens the door for Javi and as he slips in, he slides one finger across the length of his throat, laughing his way inside the Six Shooter.

And then all eyes are on Gabi before she takes off down the road.

———

"So, what's next with all this?" I ask, breaking an uneasy

silence that's taken up the living room since we returned. My eyes land on Gabi, as does everyone else's around me, and she doesn't say anything.

"I have a plan. It'd involve robbing cash trucks. Three cities… one day," Shane says, breaking the silence and scanning the room. "We'll hit them with light explosives… enough to demobilize them." He pauses, taking a deep breath. "And then we hit 'em. That's the gist of it anyways."

"I'm in," I say abruptly, and Paige's focus quickly shifts to me. I don't look at her but instead continue, "I'm in. As long as nobody gets hurt, and nobody finds themselves caught up… I'm in."

"Y'all know I am," Rock says, shrugging. "I reckon I wouldn't be here otherwise." Gabi mouths a 'thank you' to him and he nods.

"Here's the thing…" Irish says, his fingers still running through Brandi's hair. "I'm in too."

"What the fuck, dude? Way to be dramatic," I say with a laugh.

"Just give me my Emmy already," he says and smiles. "I imagine you're gonna need a driver for this. And I'm pretty damn good at that, if I do say so myself."

"Can we speak, please," Paige whispers and after a quiet moment, I stand without responding.

"We're going to go get some fresh air. Maybe a blunt will be rolled when we get back?" I ask, wriggling my brows and then reaching a hand out for Paige. She takes it and we proceed to the door. I grab my leather jacket, slip it over her shoulders, and we head out.

"Babe, talk to me. What's wrong?" I ask as Paige as I take

a seat on the porch step. She does too and shoots a glare at me that tells me I should know already.

"Xander, think about this for a second. You got out of prison, what... a couple weeks ago. Maybe a month. And then you left me to find your sister, and I get that, but what am I supposed to think here? When you're pretty much telling me you're gonna risk going back to prison."

I scratch my chin, thinking, and unable to come up with anything to say. I see where she's coming from, but also see no other alternative.

"It's my sister," I finally say, shaking my head. "It's my sister, Paige. Do you get that? I may not know a thing about her, but it doesn't matter. She's blood. And she's all I fucking got."

"You—you've got me," she stammers, the tears starting to fall and it rips my fucking heart out. I grab her and pull her in.

"You know I don't mean it like that, baby." I put my lips against her forehead, taking in every bit of her before pulling back. "She's just the only family I have."

Paige trembles, her face falling into her hands as she begins to weep.

"And what..." she sniffles, speaking into her hands. "What family do I have, Xander? Tell me. What do I have left?"

My mind runs and runs but comes up with nothing. *Nothing.* Which is exactly what she has left.

"I'm so sorry, Paige." I put a hand to her face and pull her eyes to mine. "Just like I would fight to the ends of the earth for you... I will for her too. I'm sorry. There's just no other way around it."

"I get it," she sighs, her eyes still toward the ground.

"Baby, I love you so much," I say sincerely, drawing her eyes to mine. "You mean the fucking world to me. Just please..." I pause, taking a deep breath. "Please understand that I have to do this. I have to help."

She doesn't say anything for a moment, letting my words linger in the air.

"Just promise to come back to me," she says, her head leaning into my chest.

"I promise," I say, brushing the hair from her eyes. "I promise I'll be back, my love." As I admire her gorgeous face under the moonlight, a single tear rolling down her cheek, our moment is disrupted by the thump of a bass drum, then another and another. A snare drum kicks in and then a bass line after that. The vibrations carry out to the porch with ease through the rickety front door.

"What the fuck?" I say, my face scrunched and focused on the door.

"Go in, babe," Paige says, standing and motioning for me to do the same.

I do and we walk in, the reverb from the amp hitting us hard as we enter and the thump of the bass drum setting a cadence.

"What the fuck? Who plays the drums?" I repeat, catching Gabi on the couch, in mid conversation with Brandi.

"Rock does. He and Shane used to be in a band together," Gabi replies.

"Well shit, I want to," I say, my focus still on the guest room door where the sound is coming from.

"Hey, there's another guitar in there," she says. "Go ahead."

"Your neighbors don't care?" I ask, inching my way toward the guest room.

"Shit. There're gun shots and hood music ringing all night long around here. They won't even flinch."

It's all I need to go in the room and join them.

CHAPTER FIFTEEN

Gabriela

"When I Go"—The Wild Reeds

IT'S NOT OFTEN I FIND MYSELF IN A ROOM WITH ONLY WOMEN. In fact, over the past decade or more of my life I can't remember a time when I was; let alone in my own house with two complete strangers. Knowing I should probably play kindly host, my mind runs through conversation topics. I spin the wheel and unleash the word vomit.

"How long have you been seeing Xander?" I ask, my voice raised over the live music in the background. I hand out beers I retrieved from the fridge. First, to Paige on the loveseat, then to Brandi on the recliner before spreading out on the couch myself.

"Well, that's an interesting question," she says, a soft giggle following. "We first met over three years ago. But we lost touch for a while." She slips her bottom lip between her teeth, her focus shifting around the room, before she finally turns to me. "We reconnected a few months ago. What about you and

Shane? How long have you been together?"

I laugh, waving a hand. "No, no… we dated, or whatever you wanna call it, a while ago… back in our early days. We're just friends now though. Best friends," I correct myself. "The poor guy loves me though. I think we're just too good of friends at this point."

"You don't love him back?" Paige asks.

"Oh, well, I mean, of course I love him. He means everything to me. Let's just say I'm indefinitely off the market."

"I get it," Paige says, nodding.

"What about you? What's your story?" I motion toward Brandi and she raises her left hand, wiggling her ring finger before setting it back to her lap.

"Chase and I have been married a few months now. Just did the courthouse thing. He still owes me a damn honeymoon." She squints, pursing her lips. "Shithead." She smirks, lifting her beer. "You got anything stronger by the way? That was a shit ride today. I'm trying to get stupid."

I laugh, nodding my head. "You got it." I stand and walk to the kitchen. Grabbing a bottle of Fireball and Jack Honey from the fridge, I return with them and hold them up, asking, "Will this do the trick?"

Brandi licks her lips and reaches her hands out with gimmie fingers. She snatches the Fireball and takes a stiff chug directly from the bottle. She passes it to me and I follow suit.

"Much better," Brandi says, fighting off the aftertaste as I pass the bottle off to Paige. I take a seat back on the couch and stow the Jack Honey on the coffee table.

Paige takes a small sip and sets the bottle down beside the other. She then looks at me, concern so thick in her brow you could detect it from a mile away.

"This plan of yours… do you think it'll work?" she asks.

"First off, this isn't my plan. I didn't want to involve other people. This is Shane's baby. My plan was to say fuck it and rob some bank a county over or something." I chuckle and shake my head at just how stupid that plan would be. "Do I think his plan can work?" I continue. "Yeah, for sure. Shane knows more about explosives than anyone…" I stop myself, taking another shot from the Fireball bottle as I think about all the other secondary things that could send even his plan to shit… and fast. "Can I say a police officer or patrolman won't be driving by at that exact moment… that one of the IEDs won't detonate at the wrong time, hitting another vehicle instead… Or that the cash truck driver may not be wearing a seat belt and hits his head in such a way that it kills him… no, I can't say that. I'm a realist. And being a realist, I know there are a million different things that could go wrong."

Brandi and Paige both look at me as if I just dropped a bomb on them. And maybe I did. I don't know their past. I don't know if they can understand the reality of a situation like this. But the truth is all I know. A tear rolls down Paige's cheek, but she catches it with her hand quickly as she looks away.

"I don't mean to be so doom and gloom," I say, smiling. "There're three of us here who served several tours with Special Forces. We can make this happen." I take a deep breath, straightening up a little on the couch. "Everything just has to go right."

Paige shakes her head slowly. "It's all just so crazy… so damn crazy."

"Tell me about it," I say flatly. "It's not an ideal situation. And I promise you, I've told Xander I don't want or need his help. I don't want him risking his ass for me any more than you do." Her apologetic eyes meet mine.

"No, I didn't mean it like that—"

"She's been through a lot lately. I think this is hard for all of us to process," Brandi says, cutting Paige off and passing her a remorseful look.

"It's okay, Brandi," Paige says, putting her hand up. She looks at me, her hands clasping together. "I love Xander... with all my heart. And I only want what's best for him. And trust me, what's best for him right now is doing whatever it takes to help you. He's been hurting over this... this situation for a long time."

"We'll be okay," I say, shaking my head slowly. "Everything will be okay."

———————

As the sun rises, I monitor my phone like a hawk while also watching Shane snoring in bed beside me. I haven't slept all night, worried about what we are all about to take on and how many lives are now involved. I was drunk, sobered up, and got drunk again and my eyes now burn. My eyelids fight to close, but when they do my mind just runs. I need a fix. And I need one now.

My guy has a no morning text rule, but he knows if I do message him as early as I did this morning that I'm fiending hard. Being a childhood friend and all, my last one left in this God forsaken town, he takes care of me when he can. The two hours I've waited now for his happy ass to get back to me is mind numbing. I certainly have time, as Shane and the other guys played well into the night with an adequate amount of liquor breaks. Rock took off sometime during the night to meet his boy toy, but the others stayed up drinking into the early morning hours.

The girls and I stayed up too, talking about our pasts, and learning that we have more in common than maybe I originally thought. Paige is so timid when you first meet her. An immediate thought, as in my case, can obviously sway toward weakness. But she's far from it. I was shocked to hear what she's had to overcome. It makes me feel selfish about involving her and Xander in my self-induced downfall. By the time everyone racked out, the quiet loneliness that was left and an unstoppable bout of insomnia led me to here—to this yearning.

My gaze drifts to the vanity directly across from me, catching my sad reflection. I scowl back at the ugliness I see. The desperate state of an ill-fated woman. I brought all of this on myself. And now so many others are risking everything to help me dig myself back out. It's fucked. It's all just so *fucked*.

The phone, clutched tight in my hands, finally goes off and I quickly bring up the message.

Ricky: Yeah, I got you. Meet you in fifteen. Usual spot.

I pocket my phone, the surge of anticipation buzzing inside me. I can nearly taste it. I move as quietly as I can, from my bed to the closet and slip on a pair of chucks. Shane tosses in his sleep, muttering something, and I freeze completely, glancing back to find he's still fast asleep, battling a nightmare as usual. I open the door slowly and creep out, shutting it as quietly as I can. I slink through the front room, stepping over sleeping bodies sprawled out on the floor. I slip out the front door, shutting it behind me and not bothering to lock it as it's only a short walk away. Starting up the Harley engine now would be much too loud anyway.

It's always sobering to walk in the early morning light after a night of drinking on no sleep. It feels almost like a lucid dream. Like your body is there, but your mind is adrift in the clouds. The warmth of the rising sun hits my skin in a way that makes me wish I could post up right here on the sidewalk for a quick catnap. I spot Ricky in the distance, though, leaning against a dead end sign. He smiles as he spots me and gives a quick wave. The houses around us are desolate and wasting away in varying degrees of degradation. This neighborhood, like many throughout Trinity, has gone to shit. It makes for a good drug deal spot because of it though. It also makes it odd that there's a van parked on the street. Normally, I'd investigate it further, but in my half-dazed state, the one and only thing I truly care about is getting my hands on some coke. When I'm just a few steps away from him, Ricky's demeanor changes. His smile fades and lines take up his forehead.

"I'm so sorry, Gabi," he mutters, shaking his head, his eyes falling to the pavement. "I'm so sorry."

I feel hands wrap me up, causing me to thrust my head back in reaction. I feel a thud and the arms release me. Turning, I see I've cracked open the nose of one of Javi's guys. A few more pile out of the van, and as I go to run, the van darts toward me, the engine revving. I change direction just in time to run into Javi himself, my chin meeting his thick chest. I take a step back, but it's too late. Smiling, his gold tooth shimmering in the early sunlight, he thumps me in the head with a blackjack... and darkness takes hold.

CHAPTER SIXTEEN

Xander

"The Water"—Fossil Collective

"FUCK!" A VOICE, WHAT SOUNDS TO BE SHANE, RIPS through the house. Paige nudges me until my eyes open again.

"Motherfuckers!" he yells again, so loud it's as if the guest room door isn't even shut.

"What's going on?" I mumble, my eyes adjusting to the sunlight.

"Your guess is as good as mine. Doesn't sound good though," she says as I turn over and look at the clock. I painstakingly climb out of bed with a groan as the guest room door comes tearing open. Shane stands, a note in his hand and his face flushed bright red.

"Read it," he says, handing it out for me to take. I grab it, rubbing a finger and thumb in my eyes before beginning to read.

I'm glad so many of Gabi's friends have come to play. This

*must mean there are more than enough pockets to cover her debt.
For our troubles, another 50K has been added on. That makes
150K total. You have five days now. In five days, if I don't have
my money. She dies.*

*When you have the money, leave a note for us on the back
of the dead end sign off Gladney St. After that, we'll leave instruc-
tions at the same spot.*

I drop the note to my side, my head shaking. "That motherfucker," I say, handing it back over to Shane who storms back
out of the room with it. Paige and I follow behind him and see
Brandi sitting with Irish on the couch, concerned looks on their
faces.

"When the hell did this happen?" I ask.

"I have no clue," Shane replies, running his hands through
his hair as he paces the room. "I woke up and she wasn't in bed
with me. I went outside to see if her bike was gone and this shit
was taped to the fucking door." He lifts the note, shaking it before tossing it to the ground.

"Well, they certainly didn't take her from the house. One
of us would've woken up," Brandi says.

"She was probably smoking or something," Shane responds. "Fuck! I should've just taken her with me to Seattle. We
would've had a better chance than staying here. Goddamn it."

"Well, what if we see your plan through. We can do it without her. And you said there's enough in the three trucks to pay
them off, right?" I ask.

He nods. "Yeah, should be. Should be enough for the full
one-fifty."

"So, then we continue forward as planned. What else can
we do?" I ask, shrugging.

"Anybody know where this fucker lives?" Irish asks.

"Nah, nobody knows a thing about this motherfucker. Or they just aren't willing to talk," Shane says, scratching his beard. "Jimmy may know something though, might be worth a shot, but I say we continue forward as well. So, I'll be breaching, and Rock's going to be our point man. Who wants to snatch the loot?" he asks, scanning the room.

"Well, I'm driving… And Brandi, baby, I'm sorry, but you're staying back," Irish says, and Brandi backhands his arm in response. He draws back, rubbing the same arm. "Damn, woman!"

"Don't boss me around then," she says, shrugging.

"I just don't want you involved on this level, Brandi. I don't want anything happening to you." He wraps an arm around her and she glances up at him.

"And you think I want something happening to you?" she asks, rhetorically.

"Honestly, we need someone on lookout anyways. Pig patrol," Shane says, looking at Brandi. "If you wouldn't mind that is." She nods and then shoots a dirty look at Irish before poking him with a playful elbow.

"I'll do it," I say before taking Paige's hand in mine. "And I'd like you to stay back with Brandi too, babe. Please?" She nods, leaning in for a kiss which I happily oblige.

When she takes her lips away from mine, she looks me in the eyes without a word, as if hoping to pass something on to me. "Be safe. Just be safe," she whispers.

"I promise, baby," I whisper back and take her hand to my lips, kissing the back of it before directing my attention back to the room.

"So, when?" I ask, and Shane finally stops pacing.

"Three days from now. The trucks will be right where we need them on Thursday," he says, letting out a slow exhale.

"Two days before it's due?" I ask, shaking my head and my mind running wild. "Fuck it. Okay, so Thursday it goes down. Thursday, we get Gabi back," I say, hoping no one detects my complete uncertainty and fear.

"You gotta be shittin' me," Jimmy says, leaning against the bar top.

"Not one fucking bit," Shane mutters between gritted teeth.

"When the hell did this happen?" Jimmy asks, eyeing Chase, Rock and me before his concerned gaze lands back on Shane.

"Yesterday morning. Not sure about the time," Shane says, taking a deep breath and then glancing behind his back at the only two other people in the bar, seated at the rear and minding their own. He looks back toward Jimmy. "We're wondering if you might know where this fucker hangs out. Maybe where they could be keeping her."

Jimmy rubs a palm across his forehead and shakes his head. "Nah man. Javi's big time 'round these parts. He don't show a lot a his cards." He leans in which brings all of us in a bit as well. "I tell ya what, though. I can promise ya one of his guys will be in here at some point. No doubt he told 'em to stay away. Some will anyhow. And I'm sure you could encourage them to talk." He winks as he buries his hands into the beer cooler to top us off.

"You see any of them recently?" I ask, grabbing a beer from him and returning a nod.

"A few the night before last. Started some shit with some locals," Jimmy says, sipping a beer of his own. "Just a little secret between us gentlemen right here," he continues. "If y'all find out where this fucker's keeping her and decide to go in, I've got plenty of unregistered toys for y'all to play with. You'll go in that motherfucker like Wounded Knee, ya know what I mean?" He wiggles his brows and a brief pause follows. "Like y'all will kill everyone, s'what I mean."

"Yeah," Shane says, grinning. "We get it."

"Cause the US cavalry killed one hundred and sixty-five Sioux injens at Wounded Knee," Jimmy continues, giving an affirmative nod.

"Jesus, Jimmy, we're tracking," Shane says, chuckling. "You don't always gotta keep going with the joke, man. You gotta stop it at the punchline."

"Hey, you do you, I'll do me. Ya know what I mean?"

"You're going off track again, Jimmy," Shane says, motioning for him to come closer.

"Now, how much C4 you got?" Shane whispers, glancing at me and behind his back again, before his eyes shift back to Jimmy, who leans in closer.

"What's your interest?"

"Can we call it need to know basis?" Shane asks, shrugging.

Jimmy scratches his patchy beard, his eyes roaming over each of us before he eventually shakes his head. "Nah, I can't do that. I'm in the need to know if I'm providing the bang," he says, his hands meeting his hips.

"Breaching," Shane says. "Armored truck."

Jimmy's eyes light up. "Ohhhhh! Me likey," he says, rubbing his hands together. "Yeah, I got something for y'all."

CHAPTER SEVENTEEN

Paige

"*Black Leaf*"—John Paul White

THE SUN CREEPS EVER SO SLOWLY OVER THE HORIZON AS our rented Charger with fake temp tags cruises down the barren highway. A few vehicles pass us here and there, but as early as it is, morning rush hour is still a few hours away. Chase mans the steering wheel and maintains a tight focus on Xander, Rock and Shane on Harleys ahead of us. I was lucky enough to sneak into Chase's vehicle undetected by Xander, and after working an expert pouty face with Chase, he kept quiet.

The sharp click and fizzle of his walkie-talkie startles me. He lifts it to his mouth.

"I didn't get that. Say again, over."

"Chase, babe... it's Brandi. You've got police coming up your ass about a mile back. Cheyenne PD," she shouts into her walkie-talkie. Doing her best to overpower Rowdy's barking in the background as they trail us from a few miles back.

"Roger, thanks, love," Chase responds and sets the

walkie-talkie to the side.

"All good," Shane's voice says over the line. "We're ten minutes out. Plenty of time. Brandi, just be sure to let me know when you spot the cash truck, over and out."

My heart is racing. Regardless of how cool, calm and collected everyone else seems to be, I'm scared shitless. I've never done anything like this in my life. There's something else there too; mixed in with all the chaos and bundled nerves is an exhilaration I haven't felt before. It's a tingling sensation sweeping across my body.

"Chase, do you think this will work?" I ask him, and he glances over at me, a wrinkle of concern in his brow.

"I wanna tell you everything is gonna be alright," he says, his eyes meeting the road again, hesitation taking over. "But, Paige, you're like a sister to me. I love you to death," he says, and I put a hand to his shoulder and smile.

"Aw, I love you too, big guy."

"Well, then you know I can't lie to you. This is ugly business. Any number of things could go wrong..." His voice trails and he seems to grip the steering wheel tighter now. "We'll get through this though, right?" He tilts his head to me, his eyes landing on mine and he smiles. "Like we have everything else."

"You've got it," I say, smiling, my focus shifting out the window to the passing trees. As we cross paths with a large lake, stretching out into the sea of pines, my mind wanders to my father, and all the time we used to spend at Twain Lake. All the memories that will never be made again. All the times my mother and father proved to me their unconditional love, and all the times I'll never experience it again. And then I think about Xander, and the possible outcomes of today, him lying dead in the middle of the freeway, or cuffed and dragged to prison for good this time, and I bawl, unable to control the feelings anymore.

"Paige..." Chase says, wrapping a big paw around the nape of my neck. "What's going on, hun?"

"I just—" I take a deep breath, wiping my face of tears and keeping my weeping eyes from his full view. "I just miss my parents, that's all..." My voice trails as I allow the moment to take me away from here, away from the fear of what today will bring, away from the misery of losing my parents, to a place much better. When their smiling faces were met with a long warm hug. When Mom used to lie with me and hold me when a boy would do me wrong. When Dad would take me out hunting, teaching me all he knew, and a beaming proud smile on his face when I'd get a kill. I wish I could go back so damn bad.

"I'm so sorry, Paige. I really am," Chase says, giving me a good squeeze. "But Xander will be okay. I promise." He hesitates for a moment and then continues, "I'll make sure of it."

I smile at him, leaning into his hand when the radio cuts on again.

"I see the truck," Brandi's voice says from the other end. "Coming your way now. About five minutes out."

"Roger that," Shane says, his voice cutting out for a moment before coming back over the line. "The bang will go off at mile marker one sixty-five. Brandi, hang back a bit to keep eyes on our six and set up the cordon, over and out."

There's a still, uneasy silence in the rental as Chase returns both hands to the steering wheel.

"Welp, here we go," I say, and Chase lets out a nervous chuckle.

"Here we go," he repeats.

A few stomach-churning minutes later, the Loomis cash truck cruises past us. Chase's hands are so tight against the steering wheel that his knuckles have turned white as the truck pulls past the three bikes and continues down the road.

"It's go time," Shane's voice calls out over the radio. My toes instinctively curl in anticipation.

As if on schedule, a small explosion erupts from the side of the road and the armored truck jerks and sputters as it slows to a stop, smoke pouring from the engine. Shane pulls up directly behind it, parks, and reaches into his saddlebag. He riffles through it for a moment as we slow considerably behind him, and then he pulls out a small black object. He slaps it right in the middle of the back doors of the truck, it sticks, and then he circles back around to Xander and Rock's position. The three of them slow to a stop a few hundred feet behind the truck just as there's a subtle explosion, a burst of light, and the truck doors pop open. Rock dismounts his bike, helmet and shades still on, with a gun drawn and walks with it aimed at the driver's side window as he slowly side-steps to the front of the vehicle.

Meanwhile, Xander and Shane dismount their bikes and snatch two empty duffels from each of their saddlebags. With them in tow, they hop into the back of the truck. I glance in the side view and spot Brandi about a quarter mile back with the freeway blocked off using her rented Explorer and setting up the road closed sign we acquired yesterday. A few cars are already behind her, but not enough to raise concern, Chase is sure to mention.

We come to a stop in the rental just behind the Harleys as Shane and Xander rush out with the duffels now full. Shane calls something out to Rock, who waits for them to stuff the duffels into their saddlebags and mount their bikes before he moves himself. He jogs to his own bike and hops on and they race away as fast as they can. We follow close behind in the rental and when I look in the rearview and spot Brandi climbing back into the Explorer and racing away, I breathe a sigh of relief.

A trail of us follow Shane as he speeds off the next exit and races down the two-lane road. I grip the armrest tightly as we're thrown about the weaving rental. Shane takes several turns, guiding us deeper into a sprawling suburbia just outside of Cheyenne.

"Chase, Brandi… This is Shane, over," Shane says through the walkie-talkie.

"Here," Chase says, the walkie to his mouth as Brandi confirms the same.

"This is where we split off," Shane continues. "You guys take eighty-five south. We'll take twenty-five. Back roads all the way down after that. Remember we need to be off interstate twenty-five, exit fifty-six in Ventura promptly at nine forty-six a.m. We'll then only have twenty minutes to get set."

There're okays and rogers all around as the bikes split off on three separate roads, and then we follow suit, taking our own designated road as Brandi passes us to take hers. Shane had this planned to a tee, with directions for each of us scribbled on notebook paper. I can only hope the remaining two go as well as the first.

The second armored truck, one Shane said was headed to a recreational marijuana facility and full of the kind of green we were looking for, was taken with ease south of Fort Collins. As soon as we were through, we met here off a highway smack dab in the middle of Aspen. The armored truck, last delivery of the day as Shane insisted, is on its way to a casino. It'll have more than any other truck we've taken so far. As we sit and wait for word from Shane, Chase beats his thumb anxiously against the steering wheel, our vehicle parked on an overpass.

"What's wrong, Chase?" I ask, drawing his attention.

"Busy area," he mutters, looking out his window. "Way too busy."

"Don't we have enough already?" I ask, shrugging.

"For the original amount? One hundred K… yeah. One fifty? I don't think so," he says, shaking his head.

"Isn't there another truck?" I ask. "One that's not in such a populated area?"

"Shane says no. He's been trailing them for weeks and has the schedule of every cash truck delivering on any given week within a hundred and fifty miles. This is likely our last opportunity." He pauses a moment, swallowing, his nervous eyes glancing around. "I don't think he would've picked here otherwise."

There's a brief nerve-rattling silence before the walkie-talkie clicks and fizzles.

"Fuck, guys. There's an accident up here off twenty-five. Traffic is down to one lane. I think I spot the cash truck, but it's a ways back," Brandi says. "Let me check again though."

There's a short pause and then Brandi continues, "Yeah, I can see it through the binocular thingies, but it's at a dead stop. There's a three-car pile-up right before it that doesn't look like it's going anywhere soon."

Chase scratches his cheek. "This isn't good," he says, pulling the walkie to his mouth.

"What's next, Shane?" he asks, concern etched on his face.

The walkie cuts in and out for a few seconds before Shane's voice comes through. "Let's just see what it looks like once the truck gets through. Maintain position."

Parked on the overpass with hazards flashing, I worryingly look from Xander, Rock and Shane on their Harleys in front of us ready to take the on-ramp, and then out the window, waiting with bated breath for the cash truck to come through.

"It's coming, Shane," Brandi says. In a matter of minutes, I see the armored truck barreling toward us, but along with it comes several other vehicles, speeding through the post-accident openness of the freeway.

"Fuck," Shane says, pulling his bike onto the freeway and motioning for Xander and Rock to do the same. He pulls the walkie to his face. "Let's go back," he says, sighing heavily into it. "There're too many other cars around. I'll disable the bang and head out. You guys go back to home base now." There's a click and then a short pause before Shane comes on again. "Take the route we talked about last night. Don't speed. If you get wrapped up, text or call with coordinates before shit goes down. Over and fucking out."

―――――――――――――――

Staggered, and in separate groups, we rode back to Trinity, making it back nine to ten hours later, just as Shane planned. After the necessary showers and alcoholic distractions, the six of us are now seated around Gabi's living room in solemn silence without her here. Beyond some hellos, there haven't been many words passed. Defeat is thick in the room and I can understand why. We're a little over a day away from deadline and fifty thousand short.

"So…" Xander says, letting his words linger as he leans just a bit closer against me, his hand rubbing my knee. "What's next?" he asks, his focus on Shane who has his head in his hands across from us on the loveseat.

"A hundred grand is a lot of money," Shane says into his hands before lifting his head from them. "I think, considering we're out of time, we offer them what we have," he continues with uncertainty tainting his words. "It's a lot of fucking money. I think they'll take it."

CHAPTER EIGHTEEN

Gabriela

"Hunting Sky"—Sumie

I'M NOT SURE HOW LONG I'VE BEEN IN HERE, THE DARKNESS is constant, but I know I've never been hungrier or thirstier in my entire life… and I've been through the most hardcore military schools there are. Still… this is the worst. I've been curled in a ball on the concrete floor, my hands cuffed to a pipe in the middle of the room, for God knows how long, without the strength to do much else.

I'm at an interesting little impasse as the delusions that come along with hunger overtake me. I know what it means if they come in this room… I know what will be done to me will be ugly dirty things. But I don't know how much longer I can lie here in the dark, with only my thoughts and this gripping pain in my stomach to keep me company.

My thoughts trail in what feels like a dream to Shane. He was out of the Army for about two years by the time I was getting ready to transition out myself. He flew me out to Seattle for a week and spent the whole time doing everything in his power to help me forget what I was going through for just a little bit. And when the time came for me to go back to Fort Drum to out process, he asked me to come back when I finished, to live with him in Seattle, to let him love me the way I deserved—or so he said. I smiled, took his hands in mine and kissed him. I don't kiss him often, not wanting to give the wrong idea, but then I kissed him harder than I ever have. I knew in that moment that I truly did love Shane too, but also, that I just didn't have it in me to make it work. I went back to Drum and finished out processing, and back to Trinity I went.

Now look at me. It's funny how clearly things are seen through hindsight. And as the cold floor numbs my body, I wish for Shane's thick arms around me, embracing me, making me feel protected... and safe.

The door abruptly opens, the creak of the hinges startling me. I open my eyes, but the flood of light forces them closed again. There are footsteps. Two people. Maybe three. I squint my eyes open and see their outline, but the light is just too much. It feels like my eyeballs have been doused in gasoline and lit ablaze.

"Wake the fuck up, bitch," a voice growls, and a hard slap throws my head into the concrete. I feel hands around my hips and then my limp body is lifted, my arms still cuffed around the pipe, and the rush of blood from my head to my feet thrashes my stomach. I groan, opening my eyes just enough to see Javi standing before me, leaning his head against the pipe and smiling. His hot breath on me. I glance down and see massive tatted arms propping me up.

"Gabi," Javi says, placing a hand to my stomach that makes

my abs constrict, trying to pull away. I'm just too weak. "You know I like you," he continues, so close I can smell the combination of weed and whiskey on his breath. "I don't want to have to fucking gut you. But I will." He smiles, a wicked smile, and digs his fingers into my stomach. "And I *will* have some fun with you first. You made a mistake bringing your friends here, Gabi. That tells me one thing, that you want a fight. Well, my dear, the fight's been brought to them."

I close my eyes again, hoping it will take me to a place far from here. Another slap, harder than the last, and my ears are ringing.

"I said wake up!" Javi scolds, digging his fingers in deeper.

My eyes creep open and I have barely enough strength to keep my head steady.

"I just hope they have my money, Gabi. I hope they do… for your sake," he hisses, finally letting go and snapping his fingers at another of his crew behind him. The man steps forward, a dog bowl in his hands and a can of SpaghettiOs. He tosses the bowl on the ground and pulls the tab on the can, and as he pours the contents into the bowl, my stomach growls in desperate anticipation. I can't help but salivate. I look at Javi who nods at the man holding me. His massive arms release me and I drop to the floor with a thud.

With all my strength, I lift myself up and drag myself closer to the bowl. I begin piling the delectable Os into my mouth by the handful as a water bottle is tossed my way. It rolls toward me, hitting the dog bowl as I'm closed in the darkness again.

CHAPTER NINETEEN

Xander

"Deliverance"—RY X

RELUCTANTLY, I TAPE THE NOTE FOR JAVI BEHIND THE DEAD end sign off Gladney. Over the silence as I walk back with Shane, I think about my sister, and how no one deserves this treatment, let alone someone who served. She didn't deserve the swan song she got from the Army. She doesn't deserve the mess she finds herself in now. Any combat veteran's struggle should be met with immediate and effective resolve. Her downfall is indicative of exactly what's wrong with the system.

"You okay?" Shane asks, swatting a hand across my arm.

I look over and smile. "As okay as I can be," I say, my thoughts owned by Gabi's status as I'm sure his are too.

"We're going to get her back, man. Seriously." He waits until my eyes meet his and then he continues. "I'll make sure of it."

"Why are you two not together, man?" I ask and he laughs.

"I'm not sure if you noticed or not, but she's got quite the tough exterior. She's hardened."

"Yeah, I've noticed," I respond with a chuckle.

"But for that same reason she's not with me, she'll make it through this shit. She's a tough SOB. Toughest person I know. When her mind is made up, it's made up."

"I wish I could get to know the side of her you do," I say.

"It takes time," he says as we reach the porch steps. Just before taking them, he stops and turns toward me. "But when you do get to know her. I mean really get to know the kind of person she is… you wonder why she was ever dealt the hand she was."

"Have you tried for more with her?" I ask and he laughs.

"Time and time again, my friend. It's just not there for her. What she's been through, she'll likely never fully recover from. I'm here because regardless of that, I love that woman more than anything in this God forsaken life and I would do anything for her," he says, his eyes red and glistening.

"We're going to get her back, Shane. I just—" I pause a moment, collecting my thoughts as I head to the door, opening it and holding it for him. He enters and glances back, waiting for me to continue. "I can't have it any other way," I say, shaking my head and forcing away the morbid thoughts trying to ravage my brain.

When we walk in, there's an uncomfortable silence between everyone in the living room. Irish sits with Brandi on the loveseat, Paige and Rock are on the couch, and they're all intently watching the news.

"What's up?" Shane asks, directing his attention to the screen as I do the same. They don't even have to answer. The smoldering cash truck on the screen says more than enough.

Rock points, eyes still locked on the screen. "Shit just got real." He lets out a deep breath and then catches my glance.

"Any word about witnesses? Possible suspects? Anything like that?" I ask and Rock shakes his head.

"Nothing yet, other than vehicle type. But we planned for that," he says, smirking.

The rentals were, in fact, rentals, but rented under identities of people who have long since been dead. To be a fly on the wall when the detectives figure that one out.

"Anyone make out the Harleys?" I ask, taking a seat on the couch beside Paige who greets me with a kiss to the cheek.

"No, we were too far ahead of the road closed sign for anyone to make us," Irish responds, his hand resting on Brandi's knee. She has a worried look on her face and I don't blame her. "No doubt about that, but you sure we scrubbed the rentals good enough?"

"One hundred percent," Shane says, standing still and rubbing his chin as he analyzes the screen. "They'll never find them anyways. They're way out in the middle of fucking nowhere." He takes in the TV a moment longer as silence sits among us. He then turns, a hand to his chin, and a smirk tugging at his lips. "I've been planning this for weeks. We're solid."

"What about the money?" Brandi asks, looking up at Shane and his demeanor instantly changes.

"I don't know," he responds, shaking his head. "I can only hope they take it. I think in the meantime, we need to find one of Javi's guys."

"I agree," Irish says, putting a finger up.

"Then what?" I ask, Shane's eyes meeting mine.

"Then we make him talk," he says. "We find out where she is… and we weigh our options."

"Is there a way to get the police involved? To have them

help find her?" Paige asks and Shane laughs.

"Been there, done that. The police don't give a fuck. A drug pusher was taken by her former boss. That's not at the top of their to-do list," Shane says, scoffing at the idea.

"It's a worthy suggestion," I say, his eyes meeting mine. "I agree, it's not likely, but this isn't a game many of us have played."

He nods, his facial expression softening a bit. "No, you're right. I'm sorry. It's just Gabi went to the police when she was initially threatened and they literally laughed her out of the place. It's a small department they got here with a whole lot of bad shit going down." Shane takes a moment, pacing the foyer with his hands in his pockets. "They don't give a fuck about Gabi. We're in this alone."

"So, they don't take the money and threaten to kill her. Then what?" I ask, and Shane finally stops pacing. He looks me dead in the eye, the news playing behind him, still running through the mess we made yesterday, and he smirks.

"We figure out where they are and we storm the motherfucker."

CHAPTER TWENTY

Gabriela

"By the River"—Stu Larson

MY WILL IS ON LIFE SUPPORT. MY ABILITY TO TELL THE difference between night and day, dream and reality, pain and hunger, a nonexistent thing. I used to think war would be the worst I ever experienced in this life. I was wrong. I've begun talking to myself... to Shane... to Xander. I see them bursting through the door so clear in my head, Shane cradling me in his arms and carrying me far, far away from this place.

I see the wide-open road, cruising on two wheels and experiencing the best this country has to offer, the sun a beacon of hope... and happiness.

I see food... anything and everything. I pile it in without concern for anything else. Pancakes stacked ceiling high, doused in syrup and melted butter; cheesecake with graham cracker crust, whipped cream straight from the bottle. I drink from a bottomless cup of water. It's as cool as this concrete floor and it tastes like it's lifted right out of a spring.

I don't cry when the opening door steals me away from my dreams, though I want to. I haven't cried here yet. Not even last night... when Javi finally took what he's always wanted.

Why should I? These are the games that we play. These are consequences we're thusly served.

I expect a repeat of last night when I smell Javi approach, a nauseating combination of cheap aftershave and BO. My eyes remain tightly closed as I lie on my side, my arms stretched out and aching from the cuffs that keep me restrained. He stops just before my head. I can feel his boots mere inches from my face. I beg he puts an end to it all... right here. *Right now.*

I'm ready to go. I'm done fighting. Take me away, Lord. Take me far away from here. I'm lifted, as usual, by steroid arms. He clutches me like a rag doll as he does, holding me at eye level with Javi, though he's hard to see in the dimly lit basement. He stands in silence for a moment, an odd smile on his face as a dripping sound that started a while ago steals my attention. It's all I can hear. I instinctively lick my lips, imagining the leak belongs to a faulty pipe just moments from bursting and filling the room with water I'll then chug with reckless abandon.

"Gabi..." he says, letting my name hang in the air and then he tsks. "Gabi, Gabi, Gabi... your friends let me down." He lets out a wry chuckle glancing back at one of his crew standing behind him before his dark eyes drift back to mine. "They let *you* down."

I smile, thankful that my time has come, that the Lord has heard my prayers and is ready to take me home.

As if I could be so lucky.

"You shouldn't be smiling, Gabi. You're not gonna like this one bit." He pulls a small switchblade from his pocket as the big man returns me to the ground, pinning my left arm flat against the concrete floor. As my foggy mind puts two and two together, I feel the sharp blade break skin, hot-like flames peeling back the layers in my knuckle. I scream out but don't make a sound. The weight of the steroid freak is too much to move. I fight to breathe under the pressure.

The knife meets bone and I can feel the separation of my finger from its socket. The agony is too much. My eyes roll in the back of my head as I lurch and writhe on the concrete floor. And I wish for death. I plead for it. In my head, at least. Who knows what's real anymore. Except this awful pain, of course. As steroid freak lights up a Zippo and sets it to my bloody nub, peeling the skin around it back, a relentless shooting pain surges throughout my hand and up my arm.

This pain is the realest thing I've ever felt.

CHAPTER TWENTY-ONE

Xander

"Revenge"—Chevelle

THERE'S A LOUD KNOCK AT THE DOOR AND SHANE LOOKS curiously at Irish and me, seated on the couch across from him.

"Ladies with the food, maybe? You gave them a key though, didn't you?" Shane asks, setting the stack of money he's holding into a half empty briefcase. Piles of twenty-dollar bills line the coffee table waiting to be put into cases as well. I've never hated the sight of money so much in my life. Never thought I could.

"Yeah, I did," I say when another loud knock sounds.

Just as Shane is about to get up, Rock comes back from the bathroom. There's a screeching of car tires against pavement.

"I got ya, Shane," Rock says, a wrinkle in his brow, and he puts a hand up to still him. He proceeds to the door and opens it wide, stretching his head out and looking from side to side. He then looks back in with wary eyes. His focus drops to the porch, he pauses for a moment and then squats. A moment later, he stands back up with a small package in his hand, an all-white rectangular box with a red bow. He turns slowly, his eyes analyzing the box still. Irish sets a stack of bills to the side and stands up. Maneuvering around mounds of twenties on the floor, he runs out the door.

Rock sets the package down on the coffee table, balanced on a few stacks as Shane and I scoot closer, eyeing the box ourselves. A gripping fear takes hold. A desperate understanding that this isn't good. Not one fucking bit. There's a small envelope taped to the lid of the box and Shane snags it, holding it in his hands for a moment before pulling out a folded note. He opens it and glances up at me, concerned.

His eyes trail back to the note and he clears his throat before reading it aloud, "You knew the price. You knew the terms. Your hands are stained. Not mine. You'll leave the amount you do have at 4356 Hickory rd. It's an abandoned house. Leave the money in the kitchen pantry. You'll then have four days to get the remaining fifty thousand. You play any games and she fucking dies. For each day it takes, she loses a finger. Ball's in your court."

Shane looks up, his eyebrows darting and gaze fixed on nothing in particular. He tosses the note to the floor and drops his head in his hands, running his fingers through his hair.

"*Fuck!*" he yells, his hands gripping at his hair, arm veins looking like they may burst from his skin. I snag the note from the floor and read it myself, for no other reason than to absorb the reality of it all. To understand exactly what the implications are here.

Shane lifts his head, his fingers running from his forehead down his cheeks and then they drop to his side as he eyes the box, dread overtaking his face.

"You want me to, brother?" I ask him, setting a hand to his shoulder. He looks at me, appreciation in his eyes and shakes his head.

"No, man," he says, his voice quivering. "I got it."

Shane lifts the box slowly as Irish comes back through the door in an all-out sweat. He staggers over, standing next to Rock and joining the rest of us in dreaded anticipation of what's to come. Setting the box on his lap, Shane slowly lifts the lid and tosses it to the floor, exposing a few sheets of white tissue paper, dotted throughout with crimson droplets. Tears creep down Shane's face as he picks the paper out one wad at a time, dropping them to the ground until he sees it... until we all see it. A finger. *Gabi's finger*, severed at the joint, on a bed of blood-soaked tissue paper.

"Jimmy, we need the toys. And I'm not kidding around here," Shane whispers to Jimmy, who's leaned over onto the bar. Rock, Chase and I take seats at stools around Shane.

"What the fuck happened?" Jimmy asks, bewildered.

Shane begins to speak, but gets choked up. He takes a deep breath and says, "They cut off her fucking finger, Jimmy. Left it in a gift box on her front fuckin' porch for us."

Jimmy is wide-eyed, anger setting in. "You gotta be shittin' me."

"Not shitting you, Jimmy. And they're gonna take another one for each day we don't have the rest of the money," Shane says, shaking his head and rubbing a palm into his temple.

"Can you get the money?" Jimmy asks.

"We're beyond that," Shane says, blank-faced.

"Shane, it may be—"

"Jimmy," Shane says, cutting him off. "I'm done playing their game. For all I know, we give them the rest and they kill her anyway. Fuck that. It's on my terms now."

"And what're your terms?" Jimmy asks, his eyes roaming each of us.

"We kill them, Jimmy..." Shane says, his voice trailing for a moment before he continues. "We kill every last fucking one of them."

"You're gonna need quite the armory. And you're gonna need to know where this fucker has her," Jimmy says, rubbing his chin.

"Hey, y'all!" he yells to the three other patrons playing cards near the front doors. "Bar's fuckin' closin'. Tab's on me. Get the fuck on out." The three grumble, but do as he asks, shuffling out of the place slowly. Jimmy walks around the bar and to the front door, latching it behind them. He meanders back over to the bar, and nonchalantly pulls a Jack Daniels bottle down as if he's going to knock it off the shelf, but when he backs his hand away, the bottle stays put, sitting at an angle. There's a loud groan and then the liquor shelf begins to creak open like lateral blinds being drawn. Behind it lays more weapons than any human should ever own, each set into its own custom green felted slot. There's an M4 assault rifle, a fifty-caliber sniper rifle, three different styles of AK-47s, several grenades, and more hand guns than a platoon would even need.

He grins at our awestruck faces. "This is just the beginning, gents." He smiles, motioning to the utility closet door beside the bar. "Ya oughta take a look down in the treasure trove and I may have a few surprises for ya."

Jimmy leads us down some rickety wooden stairs once we pass through the utility closet door, the area dark around us. He reaches the bottom and flips the light and I look to my right to see a large concrete basement, the smell damp and musty. There're rows and rows of weapons on black metal racks and it's unlike anything I've ever seen.

"Holy fuck," Shane mutters as we join Jimmy at the bottom of the stairs. He grins, putting a palm up for us to proceed.

"Go'on, gents. Check out the goods," he says with a laugh.

"I wish the ladies were here to see this," Irish says and I nod in agreement, my eyes still fixed on the arsenal as I walk slowly forward.

"Ahhh, best they aren't," Jimmy says with a chuckle and we eye him curiously.

"Fuck, Jimmy, you weren't kidding," Shane says, scoping out a stack of wooden boxes in the corner labeled EXPLOSIVES. "You got everything we need and then some. How the hell long have you been collecting?" he asks. "You got enough shit here to blow up this whole damn town."

"Well, shit…" Jimmy looks at the ceiling as if in thought and taps at his chin. "Damn near ten years since I bought the place."

"Christ," Shane mutters, observing what looks to be rocket-propelled grenades. Jimmy taps me on the shoulder and motions to the door.

"I told y'all I got a present for ya too," he says, grinning, and Shane eyes the door curiously.

"And what kind of present would that be, Jimmy?" Shane

asks as Jimmy steps up to the door and places a hand on the knob.

"Why don' ya see for yerself?" He winks and turns the knob, pushing the door open. He takes a few steps into the pitch-black room and flips a switch that floods the room with light.

Dead in the center of the bedroom-sized storage closet are two men, duct taped to metal folding chairs, with sand bags over their heads. They squirm in their seats, but to no real effect as Jimmy has them taped around the legs, midsection and chest. They're seated on top of a large blue tarp nearly the size of the room.

"Two of Javi's guys," Jimmy says, walking toward them. He pulls the sandbags off their heads. Their mouths are duct taped as well and there is a desperate fear in their eyes. "They came in here all liquored up last night. I thought, hell, might as well do my part."

"How the hell'd you bag both of them, Jimmy?" Shane asks, pacing back and forth in front of the two men, his eyes roaming from one to the other.

"Well, like I mentioned, they were piss drunk. Two spiked beers and an emptied out bar later and I had myself some fun."

"Yeah," I say, motioning to their bloodied faces. "If you drugged them, what's with the blood and bruises?"

"Hey, Gabi's pop was my best friend. I may only be about fifteen years older than her, but I've always worried about her like a dad would. He was always talking about her, ya know? Always proud…" His voice trails as he looks to Javi's men, and then his eyes drift back up to mine. "I just had to get some for myself before I let y'all have at 'em. Now, go'on and do your worst," he says with a chuckle, leaning back against the door-frame and crossing his arms.

"Don't mind if I do," Shane grunts, and immediately grabs the man on the left by the nape of his neck and throws him, chair and all, face first into the tarp and concrete flooring beneath it. The man lets out a groan, twitching against the ground when Shane pulls the gun out of his waistband and puts the barrel to the back of his head. Before a thought can even be processed, a loud bang echoes throughout the room, bringing all of us back with our arms blocking our faces. As a ringing ravages my eardrums, the smell of gunpowder thick in the air, I slowly lower my arms and see the man's head split in two and a thick crimson pool of blood spreading out quickly around it. The other man screams into the duct tape, his eyes bulging, as Shane paces slowly past him, the blood-splattered barrel mere inches from the man's head.

"Now, listen to me, and listen to me good," Shane says, though it's muffled through my still-ringing ears. The rest of us in the room compose ourselves as best we can as we wait to see what Shane will do next. "I have no problem with killing you. No problem at all," he continues, tapping the barrel against the man's forehead. "But your boy here got it easy. Your death will come much, much slower if you don't talk."

Shane drops the gun to his side and turns, motioning to Jimmy. "You got a map?" he asks, and Jimmy nods, proceeding to storage boxes lining the walls. He riffles through a bunch of them, eventually retrieving a weathered map and making his way back over.

"I told ya'll, I got fuckin' everything, man. Even got a few toys for ya too," Jimmy says with a chuckle, nodding to hacksaws, nails, cables connected to a car battery, and a blow-torch on the ground beside the door. Shane observes the items with a grin as he takes the map from Jimmy. He shoots Jimmy an affirmative nod and then opens the map completely, setting it on the ground at the man's feet, away from the mess of blood beside them. Shane takes a moment, waiting for the man's eyes to meet his, and when they do, he smiles. "Now, there's an easy way out of this. With your life still intact. But you need to speak. And you need to speak fast. In two seconds, I'm going to cut one of your arms free. I'll remove the tape from your mouth, and you will tell me where the fuck Gabriela Michaels is being kept. If you tell me… your life will be spared. Understood?"

The man doesn't move, but Shane doesn't look like he cares for a response anyway. He makes a cutting motion toward Rock and then proceeds to rip the duct tape from the man's mouth carelessly. The man yowls out in pain, yanking his head back and groaning loudly as Rock proceeds to cut one of his arms loose.

"Help! Help!" the man screams, and Jimmy cracks up laughing.

"I already done told ya can't nobody hear you from down here. Stop your fuckin' belly achin'," Jimmy says, scoffing.

Shane slips the gun back in his waistband and then walks around to the back of the folding chair. He squats, grabbing the folding chair by its legs, and he lifts the chair up, toppling the man face-first into the map just like he had done to his buddy before him.

"Hey, Shane," Irish says, bringing Shane's attention to him. "Let me bat leadoff here, huh? You guys can finish it out. I have a special treat for this motherfucker."

Shane doesn't say anything, considering it for a moment as he walks back over to us. He shrugs. "Have at it. Just don't kill him."

"Oh, I won't," Irish says with a smile. He walks to the man, squats near his head, and says, "So here's what's gonna happen. You're either gonna show me where Gabriela is on this map, or you're gonna regret having not. Understand?"

"You don't fuckin' get it, you dumb fucks. Whatever you think you can do to me, Javi will do ten times worse if I talk," the man yells, hitting the floor with his palm in frustration.

Chase looks back at us and smirks. "Well, let's get creative then, huh? I like a good challenge," he says, standing. He digs into his back pocket and pulls out brass knuckles. As he slides them on his fingers, he looks toward Rock. "Hey, hold this cocksucker's arm down for me, will you?"

Rock cracks a smile and nods, straddling the man's arm as he fights to pull it away. With two hands controlling the man's wrist, Rock drops down onto a knee, pinning the man's arm to the ground. The man squeals in pain and balls his hand into a tight fist, but Rock forces his fingers open and holds his hand flat to the ground. Without warning, Irish drives his fist down into the man's fingers. There's an audible crunch as the brass knuckles crush up the bones. He howls in pain, trembling and fighting for his hand back without much luck. Irish comes down again, on the top part of the man's fingers this time, the small bones, and there's another stomach-turning crunch and the man screams out so loud it may almost be louder than the gunshot.

Irish nods toward Shane. "Hey, make this motherfucker watch."

Shane drops to his knees and grabs a fistful of the man's hair, yanking his head up. Once he does, Irish punches his fingers again, over and over and over. By the time Irish is done, some of the man's fingers are still connected by shredded flaps of skin. Others are completely detached. The man cries out, pleading with us and violently thrashing in the chair.

Irish pulls his fist back, shaking it off, and then he slowly stands, slipping the bloody brass knuckles off his fingers as the man weeps like a child. Admiring his dirty work for a moment, Irish slips the knuckles back into his pocket. He crouches again, looks the man in his fluttering eyes and he says, "Listen to me good. I hardly know Gabriela Michaels. She's pretty much a stranger to me. So, what the fuck do you think her brother and best friend have in store for you?"

Irish scoffs, shaking his head as he stands back straight. "I sure hope you talk. It'd be a damn shame to torture you all goddamn night just to end up killing you."

Rock fires up a blowtorch, and the distinct sound sends the man into an all-out panic. The smell of urine quickly fills the room. Shouting over his cries, Shane says, "And we'll take all night if we need it, motherfucker."

CHAPTER TWENTY-TWO

Paige

"Ships in the Night"—Mick Flannery

"HOW LONG DO WE HAVE?" I ASK, SEATED ON THE FUTON with my hands in Xander's lap.

"Five, maybe six hours," he says. "Rock, Shane and Irish are figuring that out right now. They think it's best to hit just before dawn."

"And you're going with them?"

"Yeah, Paige. I have to," he says, putting a hand to my cheek. "But everything will be okay, babe. This Javi guy doesn't have as many men there as Shane thought he would. Shane pulled up the layout of the old mill online. He thinks it'll be an easy hit."

"And how do you know, Xander? How do you know the guy just wasn't setting you up?" I ask, my hands trembling in his.

"Paige, this guy would've given us his mother's head on a platter. Trust me. He was telling the truth. Besides, he's still in Jimmy's basement if anything goes down." He cracks a smile and I just roll my eyes, pulling my hands back.

"I'm glad you think this is funny, Xander. I'm scared shit-less over here worried I'm going to lose the only thing I've got left and you're making jokes."

"Babe," he says, pulling my hands back into his. "What can I do to make you feel better about this?"

"Let me go in with you," I say, and he pulls back, shaking his head.

"No way, Paige. Not a chance."

"And why not?" I ask.

"Ummm, I'm not going to let anything happen to you, first off."

"Oh, but something happening to you is okay?"

"That's different," he says, though he doesn't look con-vinced of it.

"Please enlighten me, Xander. How so?" I ask, and he doesn't say anything at first. "Come on, mister. I'm waiting."

"It just is, babe."

I scoff, returning my hands to my lap while shaking my head. "It's not. Not one bit. I'm a great shot. You know that. And don't say I've never done something like this before, because neither have you. I'm going, Xander, and that's that." I cross my arms, looking away from him stubbornly.

"Paige, come on," he says, setting his hands to my lap and leaning in. "Please, stay back."

I look at him again, compassion in my eyes, but with a stern tone I say, "No, Xander. I just can't. The only way I'll feel better about you going is if I go too."

He rubs the back of his neck with a stiff hand, his gaze roaming the room. "Please, Paige. If something happened to you, I'd never forgive myself."

"And if something happened to you, baby," I say, putting my hands to his cheeks and pulling him in, "I'd never forgive myself either. So, if we go down…" I kiss him, his warm lips pressed against mine, and then I pull away with a smile. "…we go down together."

"I hate you," he whispers, his eyes dropping and acceptance creeping on his face.

"No, you don't," I say in a playful tone. "Not one little bit."

I drop my head until his eyes are forced to meet mine. They're filled with sadness and it melts my heart to see him so concerned.

"I love you, Xander."

"I love you, Paige," he says, his voice cracking. I pull him in and kiss him again, our lips uniting and tongues gently tangling. I uncross my legs and straddle his lap, kissing him harder as my ass meets his bulge. I drop my hands to his thick carved shoulders, his naked chest flexing at my touch and he slides his own hands down to my ass, giving me a good squeeze. He pulls his lips from mine and drops his mouth to my neck, taking skin between teeth. I gasp, digging my fingernails into his shoulders as he lifts me up and tosses me down onto the futon. He lifts my tank up and over my head, admiring the way my tits fall out of the shirt before his lips crash against my body, moving from my breasts down to my stomach and back up. His tongue glides up my neck to my earlobe and he takes it between his teeth. I moan and wiggle beneath him as pleasure tears through me, my nipples hardening and a heat taking hold.

"I'm going to own you," he whispers, releasing a slow hot breath.

"You fucking better," I breathe out, my heart pounding against his solid ample chest.

He drives his hips into me and I can feel his thickness nearly bursting from his jeans. I tug at them until he gets the point, slipping a hand down to unbutton them as he trails kisses down my stomach. As he pulls his jeans down, he bites the waistband of my Soffes and pulls back, looking me in the eye with a hot, demanding gaze. He releases my shorts and stands, shedding his jeans, his eyes never leaving mine, and then he leans back down into me, kissing me. Making me forget all about where we are, from where we've come, and what's ahead. Taking away all my fears, my pain, my despair. His lips, and so much more, fill my body with a complete satisfaction you only really get when two people are making love, not just fucking. This is the real deal. This is everything.

His lips connect with my neck again, his hands moving to my Soffes and tugging them off, along with my panties, and tossing them to the floor. Kissing a pathway to my desperate sex, his hands move to my wrists, his fingers wrapping around them, and he holds them against the futon. I squirm against his grip, my eyes closing and head thrashing back as his tongue meets my wet clit. His breath is hot, his tongue soft and touching me in just the right spot… in just the right way. I whimper, the movement of his tongue sending surges of intense pleasure up and down my limbs. I fight harder against his hands and they grip me firmer to the futon as he circles kisses around my bud and blows his hot breath against it. I tremble, aching for him to be inside me.

To take me like it's the last time we'll ever get.

He lets go of one of my hands and brings his own hand

down to his beautiful cock. He slips it out, not even bothering to take his briefs off. He taps it lightly against my entrance, my body twists and turns. At once I need him to fill me completely. I grab one of his wrists, pulling at him.

"Put your cock in me," I whisper. "I need you"

"Fuck, baby," he gasps, slipping the tip in.

"More, I need more," I beg.

He thrusts in further, throwing his head back, and then he's completely seated, my body melts in pure satisfaction. A tingling sensation sweeps across my body as he glides in and out slowly, working up speed as my breathing picks up. He grabs my wrists, bringing my hands to his stomach and I dig my fingernails in... digging them deeper the faster he goes. He winces and then moans when I break skin. He thrusts faster, as if trying to punish me. And I want him to. I need making love to become fucking, sweet pleasure to embrace pain. I want him to fuck me like it's the end of the world.

"Fuck!" I gasp as I feel myself tingling. The electric build-up in the pit of my stomach that surges into an all-out, body-writhing, mind-numbing orgasm. As I peak, he keeps crashing into me, harder and faster, violently taking what is his. He owns me, body and soul. His hands circle my throat and I beg for it... for all of it.

He falls into me, chest to chest, and grasps my cheek as he continues to take me. Slipping the other hand behind my head, he grabs a fistful of hair and his lips connect with mine hungrily. He takes ragged breaths as his whole body tenses, every chiseled muscle in a hard flex against my body. He drops his head into my neck letting out a deep moan. Buried inside me still, he lies motionless, panting.

"Holy shit, babe," he says against my neck. "That was fucking amazing."

I turn my head, kissing his sweaty forehead and taking him in for a moment before pulling away.

"We're going to be okay," I say, trying to convince myself more than anything else.

And desperately hoping that we will be.

CHAPTER TWENTY-THREE

Xander

"Heathens"—Twenty One Pilots

THERE'S AN EERIE SILENCE TAKING UP THE VAN AS WE position ourselves just outside the old logging mill, forty-five minutes north of Trinity in the middle of nowhere. Irish slows the vehicle to a stop and Shane slides the door open, letting the dim light shine through. It's a half hour before sunrise and there's a touch of light and dew on all the vegetation surrounding us. There's a line of trees that separates us from the logging mill and makes it impossible to see through. Shane, Rock and I hop out of the van to get a closer look when headlights catch our attention far down the same road from which we came.

We hightail it back into the van and shut the door just as the vehicle stops behind us, headlights still shining bright. We cock our weapons, ready for the worst, and peer out the back window of the van.

"What the fuck," Shane mutters, lifting his head for a better view. The headlights eventually cut out, as does the engine, and the driver's side door opens.

"Should I take off?" Irish asks.

"Just hold off for a second," Shane says. "There can't be more of them than there are us. I fucking guarantee that."

A boot hits the ground from the truck behind us and I tense up, waiting for the other doors to open, but they don't. Instead, the driver's side door closes and who else but Jimmy comes walking toward the van, a rifle in his hands.

Shane immediately opens the door and steps out.

"What the fuck are you doing?" Shane yell-whispers and Jimmy just chuckles in response. "We thought you were them, dip shit." I climb out as well and Rock follows.

"Well now," Jimmy says, his voice entirely too loud. "Y'all didn't think I'd miss out on all the fun, now did ya?" He motions to his truck. "Besides, I forgot about my silencers. Would do ya good to have," he says, nodding.

"Fuck, Jimmy," Shane says, shaking his head, but a grin tugs at his mouth. "You scared the shit outta me."

"I do apologize. I didn't think to wear my make-up," Jimmy says and then motions to the wood line. "So, what in the hell y'all got going on?"

"Before you interrupted, we were about ready to push into the wood line and figure out how we'll approach."

Jimmy looks from Shane to the wood line and back, and then waves us on. "Well, let's fuckin' go then. Quit lollygagging."

He continues forward, clunking about as he does, and we follow close behind, Shane looking from him to us and shaking his head.

We reach the clearing on the other side, spotting exactly

what Shane had detailed to us beforehand. Just beyond the train tracks there's a massive early twentieth century building, wood and brick blackened with age, and two dilapidated smokestacks behind it.

Shane puts a set of binos to his eyes and takes a moment to observe the area. He lowers them and looks to us. "Only one at the door. Fucker looks like he's sleeping," he whispers with a smirk. "Rock, what do you think... two around back, two from the side, and two on delay?"

Rock nods, a wrinkle in his brow. "But who's got what?" he asks.

Shane looks around to each of us. "You and I take the lead. Hit the guy in the front while Xander and..." His voice trails as he looks over at me. "Xander and Paige clear the back. Is that cool?" he asks.

"Yeah, of course. Wherever you need us," I respond.

Shane points to Jimmy. "And then Jimmy and Irish can come in after for the breach. Brandi will stay back with the vehicles."

Rock nods. "I like it," he says. "Positions then?"

My heart races as I read the hesitation in the faces of these war veterans. I feel like I can handle this. There's no apprehension. But if they're nervous, in all that they've done, I fear I may have taken all this far lighter than I should have. Beyond my own safety, I'm worried about Paige. If anything happened to her... it would truly be the end of me too.

"Positions," Shane responds, leading us back out of the woods to the van.

Paige and I remain in frozen silence among bushes a hundred yards behind the old mill, waiting for word from Shane through our ear pieces. There are a few vehicles parked in the back, but no sign of people. I put a gloved hand to Paige's bulletproof vest and she smiles, though the fear in her eyes overshadows all else.

"I love you, Paige," I whisper. "Stay behind me. We'll get through this together."

She nods, a single tear falling down her cheek and I catch it with my finger, and then cradle her face with my hand.

"I promise you, baby. *We will*," I whisper just as a fizzle comes over the line.

"Team two, move on target," Shane says quietly followed by a click.

I walk, rifle at the ready, as Paige follows close behind me with her own rifle. It's light enough out now to see the entire area. We reach the mill, our backs to the wall, and we creep our way to the front. Peeking around the corner, I spot Rock and Shane with their backs to the mill wall as well, just beside the front entrance. Off in the distance, I catch Jimmy and Irish barreling forward to our position.

"Teams two and three, stack against the door opposite of our position," Shane says, and we oblige, slinking along the wall with Irish and Jimmy now close behind us. We stop just beside the wooden door. In a chair, just before me, is one of Javi's men, slumped over with his throat slit and bleeding out onto the grass. I glance up and catch Shane looking back at me. He shoots me a cocky little brow wriggle and smiles, his hand reaching for his belt.

"I've got the keys from this fucker," Shane whispers through the earpiece while motioning to the dead man. "I'll unlock the door and open it, Rock hits it first, team three follows, team two after them, and I'll get the rear. Nod if you roger."

After everyone nods, Shane moves to the front of the door, readying the key as Rock prepares to enter, Irish and Jimmy lining up behind him. I breathe a sigh of relief as Paige will be near the very back. Shane looks back and forth, waiting for confirmation nods and then he unlocks the door. Just as he opens it, one of Javi's men, sitting in a chair, begins to stand, fumbling with the pistol in his hand and with his face in an all-out cringe. Before he can do much else, Rock puts a round through his forehead, much quieter than anticipated through the silencer, and the man crumples to the ground. We file in, staying against the wall in the wide-open entryway, barren of anything other than dirt and dead leaves.

There are three doorways, one to the left and right upon entering, and one dead center. Just as Shane motions for us to split into groups, the door on the left opens, and our weapons instantly raise. One of Javi's men steps out, not anticipating the firepower that would be facing him, and he launches his hands in the air to guard his face, his rifle clattering to the ground, and Shane puts two rounds through his chest. He then quickly moves toward the open door as gunfire erupts from the other side. He pulls a concussion grenade from his vest as the rest of us position ourselves behind him, and he removes the ring, throwing the grenade into the room. A few men run from the room and they're taken down quickly with rifle fire before the grenade explodes. Shane motions for Paige and me to monitor the doors behind us as he, Rock, Chase and Jimmy storm the room. There're several stifled shots and some yelling before they come slinking back out.

Shane proceeds to the door across from the one they just exited and motions for the others to join him. They line the wall just to the right of the door and Shane puts three fingers up. Lowering one finger at a time, when he runs out, he turns the knob and pushes it open. Rock, Chase and Jimmy follow immediately in after him. As soon as they disappear inside, the third door swings open and a blaze of gunfire erupts from it, bringing Paige against the wall. I instinctively block her with my body when I feel a heavy punch to my stomach that forces the breath out of my lungs completely. I crumple to the floor gasping for air when a blinding muzzle flash from Paige's rifle pulls my attention. My eardrums scream.

There's another shot, and then another, and then Paige drops to her knees in a panic, wrapping me in her arms. I lie, trying to catch my breath as I watch the slumped body of the man Paige just shot being pulled back into the room, the door slamming behind him. Shane and the other guys exit the room they were searching and rush to my side.

"Is he okay?" Shane asks, concern in his eyes.

"I'm fine. I'm fine," I say, lifting myself and rubbing my hands down the front of my bulletproof vest until I feel it, the flattened round wedged in the plate protecting my gut. I shake my head, giving a nod to Jimmy. "Thank God Jimmy had these, huh?"

"Hey, motherfuckers," a voice carries through the door, stealing our attention. Shane backs against the wall with Paige and me, and motions for the others to do the same. "We will *fucking* kill her right here and now if you come through this door."

I sit up now, curling a finger for Shane to come to my level.

He squats and leans in.

"What now?" I ask him in a whisper. He scans his vicinity, and then his eyes trail to Jimmy, Irish and Rock.

"Jimmy," he whispers and waves him down. "Go get your truck. Have Brandi bring the van too. Ready them just outside the tree line and I'll radio you when to get us."

Jimmy nods. "Roger," he says before hightailing it out the way we came. Shane looks back over to me. "If Javi isn't in that room, they're damn sure calling his ass."

"If he's still alive, is that not a problem too?" I ask and he nods slowly.

"Hopefully, he's in there. If not, that's a problem we'll deal with once we get her out of here safely," he says, straightening and leaning in to say something to Rock. I turn to Paige who has shed quite a few tears, her eyes puffy and red, but she has a wide smile on her face. She rubs a hand along my cheek, down my neck to my protected chest and stomach, shaking her head as she does.

"I thought I lost you," she whispers, her voice cracking.

"Not a chance, baby," I say, winking, as I go to stand up. "Somebody's gotta look out for you."

"Look out for me?" she asks, helping me up. "I just killed a man." She nods confidently toward the closed door and smirks.

I roll my eyes and shake my head. "I would've had him," I lie.

CHAPTER TWENTY-FOUR

Gabriela

"Reunite"—Isbells

WITH THE SOUND OF STIFLED GUNFIRE AND A LOUD clatter, I'm crying tears of relief as three of Javi's men release me, moments from breaking Javi's rule and taking what they please, and they head to the door, setting their ears to it. And it's then I know he's come for me. This isn't a dream. Shane has come to my rescue, and he'll take me far away from here.

As the men are preoccupied, I pull my pants back up with cuffed hands and the only bit of strength I have left. The nub where my finger should be throbs with a relentless burn that has tortured me in this place. There's more gunfire and the three of them move back from the door toward my cradled body on the floor. One of them, the tatted steroid freak who's always holding me up, pulls a pistol from his waistband and sets the barrel against my head.

"Looks like you may not have much longer, sweetheart," he growls with an evil laugh.

I force a smile, my bruised cheeks screaming back at me, and I mutter, "You either."

He sneers at me and then motions toward his buddies. "Go check it out," he orders and the men creep over to the door reluctantly.

"Go out blazing," he demands, and one of the men takes a second, breathes in deep and then whips the door open, his rifle immediately spraying rounds. My heart breaks at the sound as I imagine Shane on the other side, lying in a pool of blood and being pumped full of more rounds.

Instead, fire comes back from the other direction, ricocheting off the concrete walls in this room, and the man falls, his rifle dropping to the ground. He's shot a few more times before the man alongside him quickly grabs his arms and pulls him in, a trail of fresh blood trailing behind him, and he slams the door shut. He looks back with panic in his eyes.

"Stay fucking there," steroid freak orders, squatting down beside me and taking a fistful of my hair as the barrel meets my head again.

Steroid freak's buddy sets his ear to the door to listen, but there's complete silence. The man turns to him and shrugs when, out of nowhere, there's a deafening blast. Light and smoke pour from where the door once was, and pieces of the man whose ear was against it are strewn about in every direction.

My eardrums ring loudly as I fan the dust out of my face, some of it already stinging my eyes. Through clouded vision, I spot steroid freak sitting still, his eyes wide, and in a daze. After a few brief moments, he shakes it off, focusing his attention back to me as the smoke starts to clear. He grabs my arm and yanks me to him. I cry out as he scoops me up, and pulls me against the back wall with him, my neck in the crook of his elbow and the barrel of his pistol digging into my temple.

"*Put your fucking weapon down! Right fucking now!*" a voice cries out from the hole where the door once was.

Steroid freak presses the barrel into my head harder. "Not a fucking chance, pendejo. I'll kill this bitch if you come any closer," he yells.

"If you kill her, I promise you the worst death you could possibly imagine." I can make out the voice now. It's Shane's. And instantly I squeeze my eyes shut, overwhelmed in knowing he did come for me. He truly did. Tears of relief squeeze out from my clenched eyelids. A new strength overtakes my body.

"Javi will be here soon, motherfuckers. And he's bringing with him ten times what you got. You're all fucking dead!" steroid freak screams, his massive arm clenching tighter around my neck.

"My friend," Shane says, his voice carrying around the corner into the empty room. "I promise you, we have enough fire-power to kill all of you five times over. Your best fucking bet is sending her out here right now and being done with it."

Steroid freak chuckles. "He'll do worse to me than you ever could if I let her go, bitch."

I hear Shane laugh, and then say, "We keep hearing that, but I'm not quite believing it." There's a short pause and then he continues. "See, I'll die for that woman. Are you willing to say the same about Javi?"

As a silence sits in the room, I'm hit with the inevitable outcome. My mind plays through it all, from steroid freak pulling the trigger and ending my life, Shane ending his, and then Javi's crew coming in and killing everyone else. All of us will die and each and every one of their lives will be on me. I glance down at my cuffed hands, trying to come up with something.

I take a deep breath, spotting the shaking barrel in my peripheral and preparing my hands for what will be my only attempt. I'll have one shot, and he'll likely let a round fly no matter how I hit it. It must be smooth, it must be fast, and it can't be even a centimeter off.

I calm my trembling hands, muster all the strength I can, and I shoot them straight up with the cuffs pulled tightly apart. The rigid chain catches the barrel and pulls it off my head as my hands continue up until my elbows lock out. As expected, he lets a round go and it carries just over my head, so close I can hear the whir of the speeding bullet. He loosens his grip just enough during the commotion to allow me to work my chin down into the crook of his elbow. Without hesitation, I open my mouth as wide as I can before clamping my jaw shut like a bear trap against his flesh. Screaming out in pain, he flails his arms in the air, firing a few errant rounds in the process. I take the opportunity to turn around and face him, spitting the hunk of bloody flesh back at him. I can hear footsteps come up from behind me and voices shouting, fusing together in a cho-rus of chaos. Before steroid freak can retaliate, I lift my cuffed hands and drive them down toward his face, thrusting both my thumbs into his eyes, pressing until I feel his eyeballs cave in. I pull my thumbs back from the messy sockets and he drops the gun, batting as his face as his body writhes on the ground.

The tears begin to flow as I grab the gun and crawl with it to the wall, setting my back against it. I look up to see Shane walking over to me, tears in his eyes and a smile on his face. He drops to a knee and takes my head against his chest.

"I thought I lost you," He says, through a shaky voice.

I force a smile, my focus remaining on him as a gunshot erupts, and steroid freak's whimpering ceases. I set a hand to his cheek. "You can't get rid of me that easy," I say, the pain in my entire body starting to return as the adrenaline wears off.

Helping me to my feet, Shane takes the gun from my bloodied hand and slips it in his waistband. His head tilts and he smiles as he takes me in. "I love you, Gabi," he says.

"I love you too, Shane," I whisper. "I always have."

CHAPTER TWENTY-FIVE

Xander

"On the Run"—The Jompson Brothers

"WHAT NOW, BROTHER?" I ASK SHANE. "JAVI WILL BE here in no time." He glances over at me as he continues helping Paige out through the tattered hole in the wall.

He stops once we hit the entryway on the other side and the rest of us come together around him. "Brandi, let's go! Have Jimmy back his truck up to the door," he says into the headset before focusing his attention back on the rest of us, his hand still gripping Gabi's arm. "There're about twenty cases of cash in that other room," he says pointing to the second room they searched. "I'm gonna get Gabriela in the van. Everyone else help load up the cases. And we need to move fast."

He takes Gabi by the elbow and leads her to the front door as the sound of idling engines comes through from the other side. As he disappears out the front door with Gabi, the rest of us pile into the second room.

Once all the cases are loaded up and Gabi is comfortably seated in the van, the rest of us follow suit, hopping into the van as morning comes to full swing. Racing toward the rear entry of the old mill, we take a two-lane country road and drive away as quickly as the van will allow.

"How long before Javi discovers it, you think?" I ask, breaking the silence.

Shane shrugs, his brows drawing close. "I don't know... ten, maybe fifteen minutes. I'm not sure how far he stays from the mill, but I imagine it's not much."

"He knows where Gabi lives," I remind everyone.

"We accounted for that. I packed most of our shit last night. The shit that's coming with us, at least. Most of it will unfortunately have to be left behind," Shane says, slipping his arm behind Gabi's neck and pulling her in. Her head falls onto his shoulder.

"Where do we go from here?" Paige asks, and there's an uneasy silence that sits in the van after.

"Fuck if I know," Shane finally says. "As far away from here as we can go."

"Truman Valley," Irish blurts out, grabbing our attention. "Just as a stop off. It's in the middle of nowhere in Missouri. You guys can hide out at our place for a bit and figure out what's next."

I nod my head, the plan sounding like our best bet.

"Sounds good to me," Shane says, his eyes trailing down to Gabi. "You?" Gabi nods and Shane slaps a hand against the first bench seat where Rock sits. "Rock?"

Rock looks back and waves a shaka. "I'm in. Y'all know that."

Irish sets a hand to Brandi's lap as she drives. "Is that al-right, babe?"

"Of course," she says.

"I guess, Truman Valley it is," I say, kissing the side of Paige's head.

From there… who knows?

EPILOGUE ONE

Paige

Six Months Later

"Fields of Gold"—Eva Cassidy

B RANDI AND I STAND CURBSIDE AT THE SAN FRANCISCO airport waiting for Chase to pick us up. I'm slightly annoyed as we've been waiting here for at least a half hour already and Xander was supposed to pick us up initially. He called last minute and mentioned having issues setting up for the concert tonight and that he would send Chase instead. It's been a week since I've seen Xander and I was really hoping he'd be here.

Brandi and Chase's house back in Truman Valley finally sold and we had a good time closing out the documents, shipping off the last of our things, and saying goodbye to the old town for good, but it's my parents' wedding anniversary today and he knows what that means to me.

It's so bittersweet reaching this day each year. It's a reminder about true love… what it means to nurture it, to care for it, and to see it through. 'Til death do us part. And that's where I'm stuck, because it's hard not to think about the beautiful thing that they had, that they'll never get to experience again. I look up, my eyes squinting through the overcast sun and I let out a heavy breath. I hope they're together again somewhere… I truly do. I just don't know.

"You alright, babe?" Brandi asks, squeezing my arm.

"Yeah… just today."

"I know." She gives me another good squeeze as Chase pulls a lifted F-150 up to the curb, the large BAR SEVEN logo sprawled across the black paint in splattered crimson. To this day, it makes me proud as hell to see.

We open the doors and climb in, and Chase greets us with a tip of his cabbie hat. Brandi settles into the passenger seat and leans in, and he kisses her on the cheek.

"How was the flight, ladies?" he asks, pulling away from the pick-up area.

"Not bad," Brandi says. "There was a crying baby next to us. As friggin' always. Like c'mon people, if the baby's still shitting its pants, maybe don't fly. I don't know," she jokes, and Chase laughs, shaking his head.

"Why'd you bring the company truck?" I ask from the back seat, leaning in between them.

"Just what I had available. I don't know if Xander told you, but we're having technical difficulties at the bar with the sound system. He and Jimmy have been caught up with it all day while I've been getting the bands settled."

"You know this thing is a piece of shit, right? It needs a new battery," I mention and he just shrugs.

"Couldn't take my bike, now could I?" He laughs, glancing at me through the rearview.

"I guess that's true," I mutter, leaning back into the seat, and playing around on my phone to pass the time.

A few minutes later, I get bored of my phone and look up to see a mess of brake lights ahead of us. I let out a groan.

"Oh my God, Chase, you took interstate eighty?" I ask, leaning back in and curling a lip in judgment.

"Yeah, what, you don't?" he asks and I shake my head.

"You're kidding me, right?" I shoot him a glare. "We've been here six months, Chase. Only a rookie would take eighty during evening rush hour."

He shrugs. "Well, damn, I haven't really flown much. I didn't even think about it."

"I'm going to kill you," I say, melting back into the seat as we creep forward ever-so-slowly.

I grumble under my breath. First off, I hate flying. Second, I hate traffic. Those two combined are like a formula for somebody getting whacked. Chase looks like a good target right about now. Brandi gripes from the front seat, calling every motorist out who passes us, and Chase gleefully hums along to whatever tune is on the radio, which irritates me more and more by the second. Worst of all, Xander won't answer my damn texts. I know it's the biggest show we've ever hosted tonight, I know his nerves are running high, but he hasn't really been around much this past week. It worries me that maybe a 'normal' us is wearing thin with him.

We're finally through God-awful interstate eighty traffic after an hour or so of Brandi's relentless road rage and Chase singing along to every goddamn song on the radio. Xander finally does respond, but he's being short, which does nothing to quell my spiked nerves.

As my impatience reaches its peak, the truck begins to sputter and rock harshly back and forth. Chase looks around, checking the gauges as he pulls the truck to the side of the busy road.

"Ah shit," he says and I bury my face in my hands, letting out a groan. The vehicle creeps to a stop, and Chase pops the hood, carefully exiting and making his way to the front.

"I just want to get home," I whine and Brandi lets out an exaggerated sigh.

"You're telling me. I may just hack his balls off tonight." I giggle and she looks back, all seriousness in her face. "I'm for real, chick. It's happening. I'm just trying to decide between a hacksaw and a dull Swiss army knife."

I erupt with laughter as Chase creeps back around and hops quickly back into the SUV.

"It's fucked," he says flatly. "Sorry, ladies." There's a collective groan, and he shrugs with his palms high. "Well, I didn't really have many options, now did I?"

"We have a brand new Range Rover, you dum dum. You and Xander should've figured this shit out ahead of time," Brandi scolds Chase, smacking him lightly upside the head.

"Look," Chase says, motioning to the road sign beside us. "We're two miles from Canyon. Gabi and Shane's house is out here. I'll just have them pick us up." He pulls out his phone and goes to work on it as I go back to scanning my own, Xander's message up and my mind playing dirty little tricks on me. I don't want to doubt us. I don't want to doubt his love for me. But it's hard when life has let you down time and time again.

Shane's Denali pulls up behind us a few minutes later and Chase scoots out of the truck, making his way to the bed and he starts removing our luggage.

"I guess we should help, huh?" I mutter and Brandi looks at me, her head shaking, and she laughs.

"I don't think so. Revenge, bitch."

We eventually climb out too and hop into Shane's SUV as Chase locks up the truck. Gabi's in the passenger seat and waves as we enter.

"Hey, guys," she says with a smile, her bandaged hand resting in her lap.

"Hey, babe," I say, giving her a half hug and kissing her cheek. Brandi waves as she scoots into the seat, allowing me to move in for Chase to join us.

"Thanks, guys," he says, shutting the door behind him. "I appreciate it."

"No worries," Shane replies from the corner of his mouth as he pulls back onto the highway. "We were just puppy training."

"Oh yeah, how is that beautiful pit, by the way?" Brandi asks.

"She's a nightmare, but God she's sweet," Gabi says, looking back with her foot propped up on the seat and her arms hugging her leg. She looks so good these days, it's hard to imagine how we found her six months ago.

"Ate a pair of my shoes last night," Shane mentions with a chuckle. "You know how it goes."

"So, buddy," Chase says, slapping his hand against Shane's shoulder. "You ready for this concert tonight?"

"As ready as I'll ever be," he says, shaking his head. "Hard to imagine we'll be sharing the stage with the likes of Beartooth and I Prevail in a few hours. In our own fucking bar at that."

"I'm so pumped," Chase says, leaning back into the seat and grinning.

"Can we just get there already, please?" Brandi asks, rolling her eyes and scoffing, but a smile pulling at her lips.

"Not too much further now," Shane says, taking the exit for interstate six eighty, which means we are only about ten minutes from Diablo. Ten minutes from the bar. Ten minutes from our new home.

As we exit the highway and enter the outskirts of Diablo, I can see our bar off in the distance. It's a massive building, standing alone out among the palm trees. It's still so unreal to see. I think it's like that for all of us. We built the bar from the foundation up, the seven of us. We worked tirelessly to make every inch perfect; the world class stage anchoring one end to the wall-length, custom-made bar anchoring the other.

The outside of the bar is dark, metallic and gritty, and perfect for the rock and roll vibe we were going for. It's much different than anything else in the quaint town of Diablo. It rises two stories from the desert floor with a basement below. The four-bedroom duplex on the top story is where Brandi, Chase, Xander and I call home. On the inside of the bar, I got free rein, and it allowed me to connect with my mother in a way I haven't since before she passed. Using all the skills she taught me, I created a feel and tone for the place in memory of her, from the welded sign welcoming all to the Bar Seven, to the monstrous junkyard gargoyles guarding either side of the stage. And my dad... my dad would be so proud of the three hundred or so hand-picked wines I've packed the wine cellar in the basement with. It brings a smile to my face just thinking about it.

As excitement builds and actually getting to the bar seems like a real possibility, police lights flash on behind us.

"You have got to be fucking kidding me," I whine, looking back at the patrol car.

"I'm seriously two seconds from getting out of this car and walking," Brandi says, sighing.

The officer shuffles slowly to the driver's side as Shane lowers the window. "Is there a problem, officer?" he asks in his most polite tone.

"Yeah, you got a headlight out," the officer with an impressive potbelly motions to the rear of the vehicle.

"Really?" Shane asks, looking in the side view mirror and then back at the officer. "Sorry about that."

"I'm gonna need your license and registration," the officer says, aviators shielding his eyes and a smug grin taking up his face.

Brandi leans toward the front seats and looks out the window at the officer. "You know," she says, pulling his attention to her. "We're friends with Sheriff Hoffman."

The officer lowers his aviators and looks over them at her. "I don't give a good goddamn who you're friends with," he mutters before straightening his sunglasses, taking Shane's documents, and shuffling off.

Brandi looks to me and then to Chase, her mouth wide and lip reared back. "That fat fuck," she hisses.

"Babe, please," Chase says, setting a hand to her shoulder. Her eyes dart to the hand and he slowly brings it back to his side.

"No, I'm about to kick him in the nuts and run. No way he catches me," she says, scoffing.

Shane looks back and smiles. "Yeah, well, he has my information now, so can we please not do that?" he asks, laughing.

Brandi dramatically sighs, rolling her eyes. "Fiiiiiiiine."

After nearly twenty minutes of running information, writing a ticket, and whatever the hell else he was doing, the officer finally returns and hands everything back over to Shane, in addition to a new traffic citation.

"Now, I'm gonna need you to get that fixed." His eyes trail to Brandi in the back seat. "And you ought to mind your manners, young lady," he says before turning and walking off.

Shane quickly rolls the window up as Brandi says, "I'm seriously going to gut that pig. I don't even care if this is a new outfit."

We finally approach the bar and park right out front. We hop out and as I head toward the rear to get my baggage, Chase waves me off.

"We'll get it. No worries. Go find your man," he says with a grin.

I shrug and grab Brandi by the arm, and we make our way to the front door. Opening it, I let her go first and then follow in after her, running into her back hard almost immediately as she stops in her tracks.

"What the f—" I cut myself off as I raise my head and see it, thousands of candles taking up the wide-open bar floor, all lit and creating a pathway to the stage.

"Oh, my God," Brandi says, putting her hands to her mouth. "Look," she says into them. And that's when I see Xander in a tux and seated on a stool at the center of the stage, his guitar in hand and a wide smile on his face. There are two other stools behind him, and another with a snare drum and high hat further back.

My legs go numb as he begins to play his acoustic, the sound carrying through the room. It's a beautiful melody and one I haven't heard him play before, which is rare when you're the girlfriend of a musician. He nods for me to come forward, but I don't know if I can. My feet are locked in place, my heart racing.

"Go on," Brandi whispers, nudging me forward. As I take my first step, the doors open behind us, drawing our attention, and we see Rock, Shane and Chase enter, suited up in tuxes now as well and with giddy smiles on their faces. They walk right past us, down the trail among the burning candles, and they take the stairs up onto the stage. Rock sits on the stool in the back, removing drum sticks from his back pocket as Shane and Chase grab a guitar and bass from backstage and take seats on the other two stools. I inch forward as Xander starts to sing, the others begin playing along with him.

How am I to know
What this life is for?
I just do.
It's all for you.

So many times before,
I've crashed along the shore.
But with you,
I'm bulletproof.
More than air is to my lungs, and lyrics to a song.
I do. I love you.
More than water is to rain, and pleasure is to pain.
It's true.

The best part of me will always be you.

I'm all the way to the stage now, just feet from Xander, and I'm trembling. A single tear rolls down his cheek, and catches his smiling lips before he continues singing.

Storms will come and go.
And we'll weather them, you know.
It's what we do.
Just me and you.

But should I ever go.
And the dirt becomes my home.
Honest truth,
This was all for you.
More than air is to my lungs, and lyrics to a song.
I do. I love you.
More than water is to rain, and pleasure is to pain.
It's true.
The best part of me will always be you.

He finishes playing, the others continuing behind him as he sets his guitar to the side, his eyes never leaving mine. He walks across the stage and down the stairs, and as he continues toward me my heart pounds in my chest, the blood surging through my veins.

He stops just in front of me, taking my wrists and pulling my reluctant hands from my mouth. My tears fall freely as he takes my hands into his and drops to a knee. A shaky hand slips inside his coat pocket and back out comes a large diamond ring. I gasp, my heart thumping in my chest, and I can hear Brandi does the same behind me. She fights to keep from squealing.

"Paige," Xander says softly, the music playing behind him

making it seem like a movie… or a dream. "Since the moment I first saw you I knew it was you. I knew it could only be you and it will only ever be you." He gulps, his eyes starting to really glisten now. "Will you please make me the happiest man in the world and be my wife?"

I nod wildly, putting my hand out for him to slide the ring on, and it does so perfectly. I pull him up and he takes me into his arms, holding me tight, as our family applauds and cheers around us. An exhilaration takes over my body completely. I feel almost weightless, my heart so incredibly full.

I'm going to be Mrs. Xander Evans. And I wouldn't have it any other way.

EPILOGUE TWO

Xander

Three Months Later

"Friends Like These"—Deaf Havana

"CAN SOMEONE TELL ME WHY THE HELL WE'RE IN Missouri?" I ask Rock and Irish as we wait with our bags to be picked up at the St. Louis airport. A week before my wedding and I have absolutely no idea what they have in store for me. "I was really hoping to rid myself of this place."

Irish just laughs, shrugging his shoulders. "Sorry, buddy, it wouldn't be much of a bachelor party if we gave you the details," he says.

"I swear to God if we end up with a drug charge and a dead hooker in the trunk, I'm getting new best friends."

Rock laughs as a van pulls up to the curb. I spot Shane driving it with a shit-eating grin as he nearly takes Irish out with it.

"And you fuckers rented a van? What in the ever-loving

fuck are we doing?"

"Can't tell the bachelor about the bachelor party," Shane says, shaking his head as he hops out of the van and makes his way toward us.

"That's what I was just telling him," Irish says, slapping hands with Shane who then does the same with Rock and me.

"How is everything, bro?" I ask Shane. "I didn't think you'd be able to make it out."

He helps us load up our bags as he lets out a heavy sigh. "Well, I wasn't going to miss this."

I stop him as Irish and Rock pile into the van. "How is she?" I ask. "I mean really? I could ask her, but she's not going to be as honest with me as she is with you."

"You know, Gabi is a strong girl. It sucks we had to end up amputating, but honestly, between her losing a hand and the infection spreading and possibly killing her, I'll take the former."

I nod. "Yeah, me too." He heads to the driver's side and gets in as I do the same on the passenger side, and we continue on our journey.

About three hours of driving south and I'm ready to kill one of them. We are getting ever closer to Truman Valley and I'm a tad worried about being in that place again. If that's what they have planned. As the sun begins to set, they remain tight lipped.

Abruptly, Shane turns to the others in the back and yells, "Bag him!"

With that, a rope is thrown over my shoulders and pulls me into the seat tight, and then a bag is thrown over my head. I struggle for a moment and then stop when I realize I'm not making much headway.

"What the fuck, guys?" I ask, a bite to my tone.

"Just relax, grasshopper," Shane says. "It's not too much longer."

What's probably only thirty minutes, but what feels like a couple hours, passes, and the van comes to a stop. The hood and rope are removed and I look around a bit, trying to make out our surroundings, but I can't see anything other than a small dirt road and dense vegetation around us.

"Where the fuck are we?" I ask.

"Patience," Irish says, a broad smile on his face. "Only a few more minutes."

"You know, I'm thinking your guys' whole understanding of time is off."

"Ten seconds," Shane says, eyeing his watch. He puts five fingers up.

"See what I mean," I crack. "Ten seconds until what?"

"You'll just have to wait and see," Irish says in a sing-song tone.

"Five," Shane starts, putting a finger down. "Four, Three, Two, One... Go!" As soon as he says 'go' there's a thunderous explosion, and a burst of light can be seen through the thick forest. There's another explosion, and then another, and then sirens begin wailing out in the night air, from where, I have no clue. But the familiarity of the siren is odd and nerve-rattling.

"What the fuck is going on, guys? I know that fucking alarm," I say, passing them all wary glances.

"Any minute now," Shane says.

I'm peering out into the darkness, searching, wondering, for what feels like an hour when a loud bang against the side of the van startles me, making me jump in the passenger seat. As

I twist around to see what caused it, Rock slides the van's side door open and my eyes go wide.

"What's up, party people? Just in time," Twitch says, standing before us in his prison garb, stained brown beyond belief. He hops in, Chase scooting over to make room, and he slides the door closed behind him. Looking up at me, he has a wide smile on his face as my own is still contorted in complete confusion.

"Well, hello to you too, fuck nut," he says, patting my shoulder with his hand. "Long time no see, friend."

"Holy fucking shit…. Twitch?!" I take him in for a bro hug, patting his back before letting him go, my nostrils picking up a very unwelcome smell.

"It's fucking great to see you, man," I say as the van pulls away, headlights still off. "But you smell like shit."

He grins, wriggling his brows as we cruise down the dark road. "It is shit, my friend," he says, letting out a sigh of content. "It *is* shit."

ACKNOWLEDGEMENTS

I have to first thank the Lord. It's been a long road, and one I've veered off of frequently, but His love and guidance has never wavered. I will never forget the second chance at life He gave me.

Major David Gladney Taylor, thank you for being you and for the sacrifice you and your family have made for this country. You are in my thoughts always.

Michelle, Jake, Joanne, Joe, and Kay, thank you so much for accepting me into your incredible family. I feel honored and blessed to know you. It means the world that through such a tragedy, I was at least able to meet some of the kindest, strongest, most generous people I've ever met. Love y'all!

Pops, Brad and Britto, you are my strength. I know, without a doubt, I wouldn't be where I am today if it weren't for your love and support. I love you guys more than anything and can't thank you enough for sticking it out with me.

To my boys (and girl!), Rob, Krotch, Andrew, and Beth, thank you for always having my back. You know I've got yours forever. Same goes for my VETSports crew, Kevin, Margaret, Jennifer, Jenifer, Johnson, Randy and Bryan.

To my book family, Kirby, Golden, Michael, Harper, Heidi, Christopher, Reggie, Shauna, Mikey, Amy and of course the other R&E Frat bros, Michael, Daryl, SD and Seth, y'all are amazing! This beautiful industry has been like a second family to me and it's because of you all. Thanks for all that you do, and more importantly, all that you give to others.

To Cat and Cara, thank you for all your hard work and for taking on the complicated job of keeping me in line! You two have been game changers. It's a true pleasure to work with you and an honor to have you on my team. I of course can't forget the other 3Bs who work tirelessly to get the right words out of me. Your dedication and commitment is unmatched and so very appreciated! Thank you Jen, Holly, Jenn, Lucy, Amy, Nikki, Blue, Stefanie, Angela, Jennifer, and Kristen!

Last, but most certainly not least, a massive thank you to my readers. What can I say? You all have changed my life. Your love, support and strength helps carry me through when the tough days come. Words can't express what it means to have you all in my corner. It's an absolute honor! THANK YOU for reading and supporting my work!

ABOUT THE AUTHOR

BT Urruela is a US Army combat wounded amputee, Purple Heart recipient, turned contemporary author who has written both independent and traditionally published books. He is the Co-founder and Brand Ambassador for VETSports, Ambassador for Tampa Sports Academy, Cover Model, Motivational Speaker and Philanthropist. He currently resides in Tampa, Florida with his dogs, Kiko and Scout.